SNARE IN THE DARK

SNARE IN THE DARK
FRANK PARRISH

PERENNIAL LIBRARY
Harper & Row, Publishers
New York, Cambridge, Philadelphia, San Francisco
London, Mexico City, São Paulo, Sydney

A hardcover edition of this book is published by Dodd, Mead & Company. It is here reprinted by arrangement.

First PERENNIAL LIBRARY edition published 1983.

Library of Congress Cataloging in Publication Data

Parrish, Frank.
    Snare in the dark.

    (Perennial library ; P/650)
    Reprint. Originally published: New York : Dodd,
Mead & Co., c1981.
    I. Title.
PR6066.A713S5 1983   823'.914   82-48814
ISBN 0-06-080650-8 (pbk.)

83 84 85 86 10 9 8 7 6 5 4 3 2 1

SNARE IN THE DARK

1

SLOWLY, slowly Dan Mallett raked up fallen ash leaves under the tree on Sir George Simpson's lawn. The leaves had been brought down by the first frost of early October, and by a wet, wintry gale when the wind went round from northeast to southwest. The dead leaves were blackish, sodden, oddly greasy in texture. Even so, it was work that required very little physical effort, and no mental effort at all. It did not at all exhaust his body which, though small and light, had the hard whippiness of a plaited leather thong. He could be up most of the night, transacting his real business, without fatigue. It did not occupy his mind, which could busy itself with plans. Dan always had plenty of plans—too many plans, perhaps—mostly concerned with young girls, young pheasants, and old silver.

Dan could not imagine why the Simpsons paid him quite heavily to do something not unpleasant which they could have done themselves in a quarter of an hour, without so much as raising a sweat. The ways of the nobs continued to amaze him. The ways of almost everybody else, if it came to that. The rest of the world had an extraordinary preference for neat dark suits and little black shoes, and horrible jobs in offices, and what they

1

called commuting. The rest of the world went to bed at night and got up in the morning, not apparently realising that the hours of darkness were the most interesting and the most enjoyable—and, if your training and talents lay in a certain direction, the most profitable.

When he decided his time was up (his interior clock, usually reliable to a minute, ran a little fast at the Simpsons') he went and stood by the back door. His old cap was in his hands, his smile was innocent and bashful. Lady Simpson counted out six pounds for him. She too smiled. There was something patronising, proprietary in her smile. She was like someone smiling at a mongrel puppy. Dan reacted to her smile with a flicker of tolerant contempt, but without resentment and with full understanding. He knew he looked more ludicrous than usual. He had tied pieces of binder twine round his old corduroy trousers, just below the knee, in the fashion of Victorian yokels. They were completely purposeless. He could have raked up the leaves in his best dark suit—in bedroom slippers. He tied the strings round his trousers to make himself even more of a bumpkin than usual, even more of a quaint survival. Though little over thirty years of age, his role among the local nobs was that of a gnome, a fossil, some Georgian or even medieval vestige left behind in this rural rock-pool by the ebbing tide of time. This was what people like the Simpsons really paid for. It was also protective colouring.

"A-do thenks ye, ma'am," said Dan, speaking as slow as he had raked the leaves, his tone deep and treacly, in the parody of antique rural Wessex which he always thought must be gross over-acting, but which doubled his income from the nobs.

2

He wondered, with an inward giggle, if he should practice tugging his forelock. It was not something he had ever seen anybody do, but it seemed to fit the role he was playing.

He bicycled slowly away towards the village of Medwell Fratrorum. As soon as he was out of sight of the Simpson's house, he dismounted and removed the bits of string from his legs. It was one thing to get himself up like a clown at the Simpsons', but there were girls in the village to whom he appeared somewhat differently.

He went not directly homewards, to the cramped little cottage under the dripping edge of the Priory Woods, but towards Medwell Court. Major March's preserves. The pheasant-shooting season would begin in a fortnight. Cobb Wood was crawling with fat birds, and also with guinea fowl and half-wild bantams, the covert's watch-dogs, and with Edgar Bland. You could hardly say, in the way of grammatical correctness, that a covert crawled with one aging gamekeeper, but that was the effect. He infested the place. There was war between him and Dan, of many years' standing, known to everybody. Dan took particular pride in getting birds from under Edgar Bland's nose, but it was rarely enough he was able to do so. Edgar Bland had sworn, publicly and often in the bar of the Chestnut Horse, that he'd get Dan, nail him good and proper, fix him once and for all.

It was a point of pride with both of them, particularly since, a year before, Dan had played the trick on Edgar Bland, which the soberer part of his mind rather regretted. Edgar Bland had been persecuting him. He himself had, perhaps, been persecuting Edgar Bland. He had gone into Milchester on the bus, spent some money in a

3

shop, and come back. He had left the bus, in the late evening, crossed the fields, and busied himself with various small concerns. In the dawn he had allowed himself to be ambushed by Edgar Bland, in a ditch at the edge of a rootfield, and Edgar Bland had whooped and gloated when he found a brace of partridges in the poacher's pocket of Dan's coat.

Dan was hailed, or hauled, to Medwell Court and before the awesome Major March, a new and false kind of country gentleman, but no less formidable for that. The police came. Dan throughout gently, persistently, proclaimed his innocence. He eventually produced the receipt from the poulterer in Milchester: two partridges, sold and bought with complete legality, publicly, in a crowded shop. The shopkeeper identified Dan and remembered his purchase, and Dan said mildly that he had, all along, been telling the exact truth, but nobody would listen, and Edgar Bland was reduced to purplish silence. Major March apologised to Dan as handsomely as his rather abrasive personality permitted. The police—who knew Dan very well as a suspect, though never, to their grief, as a convicted criminal—made a sort of apology. Edgar Bland made no apology, but was understood to mutter that he'd get his own back.

Of course the story had wide currency in Medwell and the surrounding parishes. Local opinion was divided. Dan was generally liked, though nowhere trusted. Edgar Bland was generally trusted, though nowhere liked. The division was not so much between people as within people. Only Dan's mother, perhaps, took a wholly single-minded view, owing to the bitterness of her disappoint-

4

ment at the life Dan had chosen, at the way he had betrayed her.

Dan bicycled slowly along Poulter's Lane towards Cobb Wood and Medwell Court. He went slowly because it was easier, because he was in no hurry, and because it let him see what was going on in his world. All sorts of grim and dreadful things, he knew, were going on in other worlds—the worlds of the men in neat dark suits, the worlds of trains and cameras—wars and pestilences, bombs and bankruptcies, the divorces of disc jockeys, all of which Dan regarded with a sort of baffled apathy. In his world, a flock of rooks was clamorously mobbing a sparrow hawk, which twisted and redoubled like a hare in front of lurchers until it took refuge in a tree, where the rooks could no longer dive-bomb it. Dan wondered why rooks should attack a predator that could surely never harm them: but he remembered seeing them mob a heron, and concluded that they acted like a kind of mindless rent-a-mob (an absurd phenomenon he had read about, confirming the wisdom of his decision to leave those outside worlds alone). A dunnock was in full song in a hedge, as indifferent to the hysterical rooks as Dan was to hysterical human mobs: sensible bird. Dan was particularly fond of its warm chestnut and slate grey, its sweet, unemphatic song, and its combination of shyness and friendliness. It was obliging of it, too, to sing in a chilly October as it sang in April.

Cobb Wood. No sign of Edgar Bland, but pheasants in abundance. The young birds were long out of the incubators. They were in the preserves, being fattened and strengthened for the imminent drives. Like fox cubs in

5

August, they were full grown but had attained nothing like their full strength. There would be no rocketing to treetop height on those young, stubby wings. That was why Major March and his fat friends liked them. And that, in turn, was why Dan felt no twinge of compunction about spoiling "sport."

A first-class shot hitting an old cock, high, at Christmas, in a strong wind, was something Dan could truly admire, though his own pheasant dinners came by different means—just as he truly admired the way Dr. Smith, in the village, cast a dry fly thirty yards against the wind, and made it land like thistledown on a sixpence, though when he grilled a trout for his breakfast, he had secured it by more ancient methods.

As Dan knew, from years of tactful inspection, Edgar Bland followed the old-fashioned method to get his poults fit for the gun. He got a lot of unthreshed wheat sheaves, cut by hand from the headlands. He tied each sheaf with a piece of twine not round the middle, like an old-fashioned reaper-and-binder, but round the top. Then he tied the top to a stake or the trunk of a small tree, and spread out the straws to make a sort of wigwam. The young pheasants hopped about on top of the sheaves pecking for the grain, and used the wigwams for shelter. Edgar Bland kept them in the covert with plenty of mixed corn and dried peas and tickbeans. He whistled when he came out to feed them, and they came running to meet him, going along little tracks through the undergrowth. They always used the tracks. They never tried to plunge through brambles. They were as predictable as cows, and as tame as Dan's own bantams.

This was all perfectly sound—Edgar Bland had faults of character, but he knew about rearing pheasants. But he had inherited other time-honoured devices which Dan found difficult to forgive.

He had let a lot of scruffy, half-bred bantams out into the wood, not to incubate anything, or do any good, or lay eggs, or look pretty, but to make an almighty commotion if anything disturbed them. Most of them spent most of their time not peacefully on the ground, like a Christian's bantams, but halfway up trees. They were a pest.

Worse, Edgar Bland had infected Cobb Wood with three dozen guinea fowl. They should have stayed on the ground, too, but they didn't. They went right to the top of the thorns and birches, bending the slender branches under their speckle-grey weight, and spent their whole time spying at the ground, as Dan had seen old women in Milchester glued for hours to cracks in their net curtains, hoping for a glimpse of something scandalous to get their names into the papers. The theory was that the guinea fowl squawked when they saw a fox or a cat, and all the pheasants took alarm and scrambled to safety. They also squawked when they saw Dan, and Edgar Bland took alarm.

All this made the wood almost unapproachable by day. Dan could make himself practically invisible, but not to a bantam a yard above his head, or a guinea fowl six yards above it. The small hours, then, were the time to go after Major March's pheasants, and the dawn was the time to collect them. But it was tricky. To be caught in the middle of the night, in the middle of the covert, in the middle of his snares, would be much, much worse than to be inter-

7

rupted in a noontime ramble; and the birds didn't come out to feed until they could see, and when they had light to see by, so did the gamekeeper.

It all made life very difficult for a man whose mother had a finicky appetite, and could be tempted most with a bit of roast pheasant.

Slowly, looking and listening, Dan bicycled on past Cobb Wood, wishing without rancour that Edgar Bland might be crippled with a stomachache or gout. He went on to Medwell Court, where his business lay. He kept out of sight of the big house and the gardens—in spite of Major March's apology, the day of the brace of partridges, his face was not truly welcome there—propped his bicycle behind a beech hedge in the kitchen garden, and prowled under cover of fruit bushes to the old coach house.

This was a sturdy and commodious building, converted not to garages—the Major's cars were housed in the stables—but to a gigantic pigeon loft. Major March had a passion for fancy pigeons. He had bought the very best breeding stock, and bred a lot of prizewinners himself. His squabs sold to fanciers all over Europe and America, and the prices were as fancy as the pigeons.

There were Turbits and Oriental Frills and Satinettes like Dan's own Satinettes, but much better. And in charge of them all was Peggy Bowman, who was Major March's secretary when he was there, and nanny to his pigeons when he wasn't.

Dan slipped in through the back door of the coach house. As he expected, he found Peggy topping up the feeding hoppers. She greeted him with delight; they kissed demurely, like old friends; he helped her fill the hoppers.

She was a sturdy, fair girl, now about twenty-eight. Her father had run the garage in the village. She had done a secretarial course, and got a job with a solicitor in Milchester. That was when Dan was serving his sentence of penal servitude in the bank, driven there by his mother's craving for respectability and respect. He had needed distraction. Peggy had distracted him. She had a gurgling laugh and a fine bouncing bosom. She had a great deal to recommend her, but she had one terrible failing. She had something Dan was supposed to have—was believed by the bank to have. She had ambition. She saw the Dan of those days—dapper in his dark suit, educated in voice, graceful in manner, quick with figures, trusted, a man with a great future—and she liked what she saw, partly for the right reasons but partly for very, very wrong ones.

Dan's father had died of the effects of spending all night in a wet ditch while gamekeepers thudded round his head. Dan inherited some dogs, some nets and snares, and an ancestral yearning to get back where he belonged. He got back, to his mother's bitter and undiminishing disappointment. He lost Peggy. That was in the nick of time. If she'd had him, his mother and she between them would have kept him in the bank. She married George Bowman, then an articled clerk in her solicitor's office. It worked moderately well, as far as Dan knew. Now she worked part-time for Major March.

Dan prided himself on many things, and one of them was that he stayed friendly with his girls. He had had an awful lot of girls, so he had kept an awful lot of friends. It

9

was something their husbands so little understood that it was best kept from them. George Bowman would not have understood the friendship between Dan and Peggy, although really it was scarcely more than friendship, coloured by cheerful memories, and sometimes mutually helpful. Peggy was not bitter, as his mother was bitter, about the dreadful choice he had made. That was odd, because his mother had wanted his conventional success not for herself but for him, while Peggy had wanted it not for him but for herself.

Anyway, they were friends, and one result was that Dan fed his own pigeons free, and another was that he sometimes knew Edgar Bland's movements.

"What have you come for today, you awful little man?" she said affectionately, in her not-quite-posh secretary's voice.

"Running a bit low on Cinquatina maize," said Dan apologetically.

Lady Simpson would not have recognised his voice. With Peggy, he was back in the bank, even though she was mucking out a pigeon loft and he was borrowing a bag of maize.

"Edgar Bland's going away tonight," said Peggy.

"That's worth ten bags of maize."

"I thought it might be. You're a disgrace to the neighbourhood."

"Paternity," said Dan. "Can't escape my destiny. Where's the old basket off to?"

"Where he's been going once a month since April. A nursing home near Quimbury. He goes and visits an old, old man."

10

"Gum," said Dan. "Edgar Bland bringing comfort and solace. I can't picture it."

"It's somebody he used to work for when he was a boy."

"Ah, then he's hoping for something in the will."

"Yes," said Peggy.

"He's been away once a month since April," said Dan, "and I didn't know about it?"

"He's only been away in the daytime. This time he's going in the evening. So he's staying with his married daughter. She lives in Quimbury. I know all this because I had to get him leave from Major March."

"A keeper away for the night at this time of year—I should think so. Dreadful to think of those woods unguarded. It's funny, though, an evening visit to an old man in a nursing home. I thought they had them tucked up and dreaming by about six, so the nurses can go off to bingo."

"Yes. But that's the appointment they made. Or maybe he made it as an excuse to stay with his daughter. You're the last person who's supposed to know about it."

"I'm the only person who's going to know about it. Thank you very much, love. Anything I can do for you, as you know—"

"Go back to the bank, kill George, and marry me."

Dan laughed, kissed her, and went stealthily back to his bicycle.

Peggy's own laugh died as she watched him go, moving as always with a sort of elegance. His face stayed in her mind, as she absentmindedly watched the pigeons feeding. It was in such profound contrast to the faces of the two other principal men in her life—wedge-shaped, broad-browed, gentle, deeply tanned but quite unlined, with those astonishing cornflower-blue eyes which had once made her knees tremble, and that slow, sweet, sexy smile which could probably still make her knees tremble, if she let it. His was not the appeal of movie star or beef-cake idol. It was more subtle and more compelling. Peggy told herself so, in good solemn words she had got from a paperback novel.

She imagined Dan's appeal was, in fact, too subtle for most girls. Only a small minority of the most perceptive would fall for him. But there, though she was right about many things, she was completely wrong.

Dan bicycled home awkwardly, his bicycle top-heavy with the bag of maize on the carrier behind the saddle. It was difficult to go as slowly as he wanted to, to watch a few straggling swallows and martins—surely the very last—hurrying south away from the clammy English winter, and flocks of cushat-doves so dense that they looked like pools of grey oil in the fields, and starlings crying in imitation of peewits because they had flocked together for a spell. None of this was of any practical use to him. But he saw everything that went on because he was endlessly fascinated, amused, intrigued, surprised, and because these were the fellow citizens of his world, needing and using each other. He preyed on the partridge; the partridge preyed on worms; one day worms would prey on him, and it was all tidy and logical and economical, unlike the messy, wasteful world of the dark suits and the pocket calculators.

The sun was going down in a hard, clear yellow sky.

There was going to be a frost, hard, only the second hard one. No moon. Probably starlight. No wind to speak of. Sounds would carry through the still air, over the frozen ground. It was lucky Edgar Bland had an old ex-employer in a nursing home and a married daughter in Quimbury, and it was lucky Peggy Bowman was a friend with a conscience that put loyalty to himself higher than loyalty to Major March.

He wobbled insecurely along the rough track that led, at the edge of the big wood, from the road to the cottage. He frowned when he saw that his mother, leaning on her rubber-tipped stick, was feeding the blue-marble bantams. The temperature was already dropping towards freezing. That arthritic hip, which pained her and crippled her a little more every day, should not be out in the cold. Probably wet would be worse. Dan dreaded the probing fogs and the creeping damp of the next few months, because of their effect on his mother. He looked with anxiety at the whiteness of her face and the lines of pain round her mouth.

He took the bag of mixed corn from her, with the smile of greeting that hid the gnawing worry in his mind. She went indoors slowly, slowly, each footstep a painful labour. Dan fed his pigeons, adding the new sack of Cinquatina maize to the mixture in the bin. He fed his dogs and let them out for their run—Nimrod the elegant lurcher, black, almost smooth-coated, seven-eighths-bred with just the dip of sheepdog that gave him cunning, so that he could wriggle very slowly on his belly in the dark, to herd hares into the net by his scent coming downwind to them, as well as run down a full-grown roebuck in the dawn; Pansy the old-fashioned blue-mottled pointer,

13

sulky and ill-tempered like many of her kind, who could not only find and point to a covey of partridges invisible in stubble, but hypnotise every bird so that they stayed glued to the ground for that other kind of net; and Goldie the cheerful little Jack Russell terrier, by no means pure as to pedigree, but pure gold for pushing rabbits out of warrens or pheasants out of hedges.

The dogs bounded about at the edge of the wood, tidily relieving themselves. Pansy snapping at the other two when they trotted up to investigate, in the indelicate fashion of dogs, and Dan sadly compared their abundant energy and fluent movement with his mother's imprisonment by a deteriorating hip-joint.

Dr. Smith said they could operate. They gave you a whole new joint, a plastic ball-and-socket that lasted forever. You could move, walk, climb stairs. You were out of pain. All this Dan accepted. All this he had pressed on his mother, times without number, far more often than she pressed him to mend his wicked ways and go back cap in hand to the bank.

"Nay," she said. "Ye'll niver trundle me into one o' they yuge wards, wi' all the sweepens o' the streets, an' doctors that look at ye like a dog wi' a creepy-crawly."

And that was that. Nothing Dan or Dr. Smith said would induce her into a public ward to have the operation free on the National Health. So it was pain and prison, or it was a private surgeon and a private room in a hospital. That had been an awful lot of money when Dan had first looked into the matter. Now it was an awful lot more. Money had never mattered much to Dan—he lived in a more ancient way. But it mattered now. That was why he

14

had turned to burglary, on a moderate scale, with a beginner's caution, and had about a third of the money he needed in a polythene bag in a rabbit hole.

That was why he would sell all but one of the pheasants he got on the edge of Cobb Wood in the dawn.

He whistled up the dogs and put them to bed. He went in, washed, and made the supper. They had a rich fragrant soup made from the carcasses of partridges, richer for a good dash of sherry, and a sort of jugged hare with leeks from Sir George Simpson's garden (honestly come by—graciously presented by her ladyship, a gesture which had caused Dan to become quite incoherent with stammered thanks in his most extreme Thomas Hardy parody).

Old Mrs. Mallett drank only half her soup, then said she was too full for the hare.

"You must eat, old lady," said Dan. "You feel the cold if you starve yourself."

"Ay," said his mother, and pretended to eat by pushing the things about on her plate.

She said she had no appetite because she never did anything. It was true. Once she had been as active as Goldie the terrier, and her crumpled paper-white face had been as berry-brown as Dan's. The change was heartbreaking.

But as the weeks went by there was gradually a little more, always a little more, in the polythene bag in the rabbit hole.

At ten Dan helped his mother up the steep little stairs to her bedroom. He made her a hot drink and tucked her up.

She looked up at him from the pillow, her old eyes as

shrewd as a sheepdog's and as worried as a hen with one chick. Arthritis had not dulled her brain, or soothed the harshness of her disappointment.

"Ye ben off t'devilment tonight, then?"

"There is an errand to be run," admitted Dan.

"Errand! That's a saucy kind o' word for your doens. Ye trollopen or thieven?"

Dan grinned, kissed her goodnight, and ran away (as he had since the age of two) from questions he didn't want to answer.

He took off his boots, lay down on his own bed, and set his mental alarm clock for one in the morning.

All his equipment was ready and to hand, though hidden where even Pansy would never find it.

He woke punctually, yawned, stretched, and tiptoed downstairs in his socks. He put on rubber-soled boots and a heavy navy-blue sweater. He had one drink, and filled his flask from the bottle in the larder. He filled his pockets with the things he needed. They included no kind of weapon, unless the word could be used of his stick, a homemade blackthorn with a lump of lead in the knob.

At half-past one he was out of the house, quietening the dogs so as to disturb his mother as little as possible. He set off across country on a beeline for Cobb Wood, using the roads as little as a dog-fox, knowing his way as well as a badger.

At a quarter past two he was hidden from the starlight in the prickly edge of Cobb Wood.

2

DAN COULD see practically nothing, but he could remember everything.

A belt of thick mixed woodland with heavy undergrowth lay between his position and the largest of the clearings where Edgar Bland had his wheat sheaves. There was not a grain of wheat left on the sheaves now, of course—starlings and sparrows had finished any that the pheasant poults had left. For weeks Edgar Bland fed them by hand, whistling to them like so many dogs, and then throwing handfuls of corn round and about on the ground. They were terribly easy to catch at that stage—Dan simply had to imitate Edgar Bland's whistle, and in a moment he was having to avoid treading on the tame young pheasants. Edgar Bland knew that as well as Dan did. It was not a thing to do often—stand whistling like a blackbird in the middle of the covert, in full daylight, a few hundred yards from the Blands' cottage.

Then the pheasants, growing up, had to get to know their environment, and become a bit wilder and more self-reliant. If they went on as they'd been going on, they'd never fly in front of the beaters for the guns. They weren't supposed to fly fast or high, but even Major

17

March and his guests wouldn't want to shoot them on the ground, not if anybody was looking. So, needing food, the pheasants mostly came out of the wood in the early dawn, to feed in the field nearest the covert. A belt of the field by the wood was planted accordingly, with some kind of bean the birds liked.

There was one walkable path from the edge of the wood to the main clearing. This Edgar Bland, with the ill-natured artfulness of his kind, had extensively booby-trapped. There were wires across the path, at various heights, tied to various things. Dan knew where they had been, but Edgar Bland was always moving them. He sometimes hitched one of the wires to an old iron bucket, poised on a branch, and when the bucket came down it fell on a bit of corrugated iron. The noise was dreadful.

The pheasants never used the path, nor did they fly from their roosts to the field. They threaded the undergrowth by their own little creepways, serpentine, complicated, well hidden by the brambles and bushes overhead, but well trodden too, by fat young pheasants over the weeks, so that they were easy to find if you knew what to look for.

There were several methods available to Dan for getting the birds he needed.

Of course the easiest was shooting. Dan had an excellent gun (unlicenced) and a great quantity of cartridges (not acquired in the way of purchase). The trees were getting bare as frosts and high winds stripped the leaves off them; the bulky birds would show clearly among the branches, against the night sky. But a man on his own was unlikely to get more than two birds. By the time he had reloaded, the whole lot would be up and away, the whole covert would be in an uproar of indignant bantams and squawking guinea fowl, and it would be no place for a peace-loving man. On a quiet, frosty night the noise of a twelve-bore would carry to the Mayor's parlour in Milchester. To be caught with a shotgun, in a preserved covert, in the middle of the night, in the close season, as a known bad character . . .

Anyway two birds was not nearly enough. They wouldn't pay for a taxi to take his mother to the hospital.

His father's favourite method, and a good one, had been alcohol. You boiled some corn to soften it and make it more absorbent, but without turning it into porridge. Then you drained it in a sieve, and then you soaked it in whisky. You scattered the stuff where the keeper had been scattering his corn, so the birds fed where they'd been used to feeding. They got drunk. Their heads were not at all hard. Of course they were unused to ardent spirits. A drunken pheasant was a ridiculous sight—very like a man—very like young Harry Barnett the water keeper or old Curly Godden the cowman after too many at the Chestnut Horse. They lurched and stumbled and had fights. They didn't know what was going on round them. A man could simply pick them up and pop them in a sack. What Dan's father liked about the method was that the birds died happy. He said the whisky made them taste better, too.

But it was a technique for full dawn, daylight. That made it all right in some coverts, but not in Cobb Wood, not with Edgar Bland only as far away as Quimbury, and liable to make an early start home.

The same applied to a method Dan respected but never really liked. You got a lot of peas—tinned ones would do,

19

good firm marrowfats, cooked till they were soft but not slushy. You stuck them with furze prickles. Or you took a stout hair from the mane of a pony, and threaded it through a pinhole in the middle of a pea, and left a bit sticking out on each side. The pheasants tried to eat the peas, and choked on the prickles or the horsehair. They were quite helpless just when they were choking, like a man with a fishbone in his throat. But they died unhappy, unlike the ones who got drunk. There was something inelegant about the method, to Dan's mind. It was something Edgar Bland would have done, if he'd been on the other side of the fence. Anyway it was another one for daylight.

Night, silence, and a comfortable departure before full day—that was what Dan wanted: so it came to the most wearisome but the most artistic method of all. Dan would not have chosen it for aesthetic motives, but he was quite pleased to use the skill he had been at such pains to acquire.

Dan crouched down, just inside the edge of the wood. He felt about him very gently with his fingers. His fingertips drew a picture in his mind, which he matched to what he had seen in the innocent daylight. He identified, by touch, the first of the creepways, the passages out from the wood into the field. Through this door and dozens of others the pheasants would come in the early dawn, strutting delicately, long tails trailing, feet spurning anything prickly, heads thrust up and forward.

His fingertips told him this creepway was too big. A bird might go one side or the other, and pass untouched out into the open. Dan narrowed the gap with a bundle of prickly twigs, making sure that there still remained room for a pheasant to strut through.

This done, he took a small piece of cardboard from the hip pocket of his tweed coat. Each side of the card was nicked with little indentations, with scissors, to make a saw edge. Wound round the card was strong mono-filament nylon fishing line, already with a slipknot and a noose in the middle. The saw-teeth of the card kept the nylon from tangling, and made it easier to unwind in the dark.

Dan unwound the first of his snares, blessing progress. His father, setting an "angle" in such a place, would have used either wire or horsehair. The wire had to be fine and springy; it was tricky to set right, especially in the dark, and horribly apt to catch the wrong prey. Dan had too many memories of three-legged dogs and gangrenous foxes ever to want to use wire. And horsehair was not strong enough to hold a pheasant by the foot only. You had to have a little stake, or two little stakes, and set a second snare well clear of the ground with a noose for a pheasant's neck. It was difficult to set in the dark and easy to see by day. To be sure, Dan's father had taken an awful lot of pheasants with his horsehair.

Dan could feel that, beside the creepway, there was a small holly. He cleared away a little drift of dead leaves from the roots of the holly. The dead holly leaves were like pieces of stiff plastic, their points as sharp as needles. Dan pricked his fingertips repeatedly. It was impossible not to do so in the dark. The leaves, when he brushed them clear of the root, made a small dry rustle. It was a tiny sound, unavoidable, but Dan hated making any sound at all.

He pushed a finger through the frosty soil under a jut-ting piece of root. He tied one end of his nylon to the root. When it was secure, he laid his snare along the ground across the creepway, the noose in the middle, so that a bird coming out that way was highly likely to plant a foot in the noose. Then, when it lifted the foot for the next deliberate stride, it took the nylon with it. The noose tightened. At least, Dan hoped it did.

There were little twigs and a few dead leaves—the minor debris of an autumn woodland—on the ground in the mouth of the creepway. Dan was careful not to disturb them. Although he had changed the shape of the doorway, he wanted its floor to look as familiar and natural as possible. Besides, the leaves and twigs had the effect of lifting the snare fractionally clear of the ground. This was fine. It reduced the chance of a bird stepping clear over the nylon. Even in broad daylight, the thin clear monofilament would be effectively invisible, unless hit by direct sunlight. And that wouldn't happen until afternoon, as this side of the wood was the western.

His snare laid, Dan secured the other end to a whippy young sucker of hazel. This too was fine. The whippiness of the wood would give to the struggles of the pheasant, as a fishing rod gives to the weight of a trout.

Satisfied, Dan crept a few feet along the edge of the wood, his fingertips confirming the next mental photograph. Again he found, by feeling, that the creepway was too broad. Three birds could have walked abreast through it. He reduced it to a single-track road by bending down some tendrils of bramble, and pegging them where he wanted them with a few pieces of stick. Carefully as before, he took out and uncoiled more nylon. He stowed away the saw-edged cards in another pocket of his coat. He was not one to strew the countryside with litter, especially as no other poacher, as far as he knew, used this saw-edged device. It might be embarrassing if his cards were found. Besides, cutting the little nicks with nail scissors was a wearisome and finicky business. The cards could be used again, if he kept them dry and uncrumpled. Some of them had been out dozens of times.

He went methodically down the side of the wood, on his hands and knees, or crouching, or sitting down. He was cold. He found his fingers getting too numb to tie knots, and the knots that secured the ends of the snares had to be secure indeed. He pushed his hands up inside his shirt, up into the opposite armpits. He almost shouted at the shock of feeling his ice-cold hands on his warm skin. He thawed them out in a minute or two, and thawed himself further with a pull at the whisky in his flask.

Some of the creepways were a bad shape for the snare, and of these some he could not improve, not in the dark, not in silence. He filled up these holes with sticks and prickles. The pheasants would go another way, even if they had gone this way for weeks. And in the other way, made a good shape and a good size, there would be a noose and a slipknot, invisible on the dark ground, on the side of the wood away from the sunrise, away from Edgar Bland's cottage.

No doubt, Dan thought, Edgar Bland would have preferred the field with the special beans to be on the side where his cottage was. Then he could have watched the pheasants coming out to feed from his bedroom window, with a spyglass. But there was a stream there, which ran into the main river just outside the village. It was a useless stream, too small for trout. Major March let little boys go fishing there for sticklebacks. He did not really want, Dan thought, a lot of local urchins at the edge of his

23

preserves, but popularity in the village was important to Major March. That was why he gave so much money to the church roof, the village hall roof, the cricket club, the boys' club and the flower show. Dan had heard all about it, in awed but mocking voices, in the Chestnut Horse. It was all mysterious to Dan. Major March was rich enough and powerful enough not to give a damn what people in the village thought of him, as long as he kept the law and paid his bills. But like the other rich men who came out of the towns and played at being gentry, he wanted to be a bluff, popular squire. So, buying a little popularity cheaply, he let the boys go fishing in his stream. They would have done so anyway. They did not think it was really his stream, but their stream. Dan agreed with them.

Anyway, the stream stopped the pheasants coming out on the side nearest Edgar Bland. No pheasant wants a bathe before breakfast.

So Dan's thoughts rambled, like Pansy the pointer in a field with no scent of game. He could not think consistently or to any purpose, because the job he was doing took concentration. It was not like raking the ash leaves off Sir George Simpson's lawn. He had plenty to think about, but he could not think usefully now. He had to think about the reason he was operating on such a large scale, the reason he was after a big, lucrative harvest of birds, which would go to Milchester next day, by a roundabout route, in Fred Dawson's van, under a lot of cabbages. That vehicle chose itself because Fred was away and Dan had a key to his garage. There was a licenced poulterer who took a few at the back door, no questions asked, a little bit ahead of the season. They'd go into his deep-freeze, the private one in his own house, and appear as fresh-killed birds when legitimate pheasants were hanging up in the shop. And there was a pub on the edge of the town taken over by a retired Wing Commander with fancy ideas of catering. It had the menu written in French on a blackboard. The would-be nobs of Milchester, the Rotarians and the Chamber of Commerce, went there to mispronounce the names of wines. The Winco, as he liked to be called, was a ready market. What he charged for a helping of pheasant was something scandalous.

The near-nobs paid it. They could afford to. They, and the Winco, and Major March, were just as bent as villains like himself, Dan thought, his mind moving abstractedly off in new, useless directions.

At least he wasn't tired. He'd had a nice two hours on his bed before he came out, and he'd be sleeping sweetly in the morning, just at the hour when the dark-suited world was scurrying into its offices. It was a thought he never tired of; morning after morning it made his sleep sweeter still.

By half-past four, by Dan's internal clock, he had set thirty-eight snares. He had not kept count as he went, but he counted with his fingers the cards he had left. Only eight of all that he had brought. It was far, far more than he had ever set at one time before. He was moving into wholesaling. If everything went according to plan, he'd almost empty the covert. Major March could shoot pigeons instead, except that probably he and his friends weren't good enough shots to kill pigeons.

Every creepway onto the bean field was either blocked or snared.

Getting the harvest away was a bit of a problem, because it ought to be such a mammoth load. How Dan did it depended on the state of the sky when he'd picked up all his birds, and whether there was any sign of Edgar Bland. Probably he'd get all the birds—making as many trips as necessary—into the deep dead bracken which bordered Poulter's Lane a little piece back. Nobody would go in there, and Edgar Bland wouldn't put his dog in there. It was a place the lads sometimes took their girls—Dan himself had often done so, when he first discovered the joy he could get from girls and the joy he could give them—but early on a frosty autumn morning was no time for out-of-door frolics. The very thought made Dan's fingers go numb again. He warmed them under his armpits, and with another tot of whisky.

All the while he had worked his way up the flank of the wood, his ears had been alert. There was very little moving. Most of the world was asleep. Rabbits and fox cubs were asleep below ground. An adult dog-fox might be hunting, but Edgar Bland discouraged foxes in a covert to an extent which angered the master of the local pack, and threatened Major March's precious popularity. Some of the little predators would be out—stoats, weasels, polecats, rats—those that Edgar Bland had not caught with his own wires and strung up on branches in his "gamekeeper's larder." Ignorant lout. Polecats had become very rare, owing to the Edgar Blands of the world, as rare as pine-martens, and it was a crying shame to kill them. Weasels ate mice, voles, and baby rats. Just occasionally, Dan knew, they took eggs or very young chicks. But the good they did to the covert and to Edgar Bland far outweighed an occasional lapse. Dan knew this perfectly

26

well, from a lifetime lived with his nose six inches from the ground. Edgar Bland ought to have known it, too. But Edgar Bland accepted, blindly, the ignorant tradition that weasels were destructive vermin. He probably believed that nightjars sucked the milk from nanny goats, because his grandmother had told him so.

Stoats were another matter. They were vicious little beasts, killing for fun, killing far more rabbits and birds than they needed, giving off a stink when they were threatened. They'd be turning white for the winter, and then they were ermine. It was funny to think that the aristocracy, dressed up for coronations and such, wore the skins of such nasty little animals.

Two brown owls were hunting over the open fields, conversing, at a distance, with their strange, otherworldly cries. No other bird was moving. But the pheasants would soon be astir.

Dan prowled back towards his starting point, looking and listening intently, making as little noise as possible. Though he was sure he had the covert to himself, he had never lost anything by being careful. He had never been to prison and he did not fancy going. And it would be worse for his mother than for himself. She'd say she could look after herself, but the authorities would declare that she couldn't, and they'd be right. They'd put her into some kind of home. They'd have a job getting her there, but once there she'd have a job getting out. She'd hate it.

Only because he was intensely alert: only because he was moving slowly and silently, did he become aware that somebody else was out.

It was not precisely something that he saw. Though the frosty sky was spangled with stars, none of their light filtered down through the branches and the undergrowth to the ragged edge of the wood. Though Dan's eyes were thoroughly used to the dark, and though his night vision was much better than other people's (he supposed because he used it so much more), he could not, with his eyes, positively identify a figure.

It was not precisely something that he heard. There was almost nothing to hear, except the distant crying of the wood-owls. Dan's ears were cocked for any tiny untoward sound, anything that meant oddity in the wood. There had not been the obtrusive snapping of a twig, the chink of a hobnail on a flint: a little cough or an intake of breath, or even the click of a knee straightened after too long a crouch.

There was nothing to smell—not tobacco, not sweat, not gun oil, not dog, not fox or badger or even bird droppings in this cold antiseptic air.

Dan did not believe in sixth sense. He relied on the five he did believe in. He told himself, as he crouched as still as a stone, that there was no more to see or smell or hear than there was to taste or touch. He had had a nip too many out of his old silver hunting flask. He was unhinged to a tiny extent by his worry about his mother.

No—it didn't do. His senses told him he was alone. His reason told him he was alone. But he knew he was not alone. There was someone within twenty yards of him, as motionless as he was himself.

Who? Why? Did he know Dan was there?

It was not Edgar Bland, who was miles away and who couldn't have got to the edge of the wood without Dan knowing about it. It could be a substitute Edgar Bland had found and sent. If so, it was a far better substitute than any he had ever found before. They clumped about like cows, the oafs he used as underkeepers.

It was somebody on the same business as himself. It had to be.

The thought was extremely annoying.

Had other snares been laid over all the creepways? Well or badly? This other bloke seemed to be good at creeping and crawling; was he good at laying his angles too? If not, all Dan's trouble was wasted. If so, half his harvest was lost.

Dan wondered how long he could stay in this crouch, utterly immobile, without getting cramp or freezing to death. If the other man knew about Dan, was he prepared to sit it out? Until daylight? What happened when daylight came? Did a keeper shoot a poacher, or a poacher shoot another poacher, or did two poachers shake hands and divide the loot? The dawn was a long way off, but it was coming. Dan didn't think he could stay where he was as long as that, and he didn't want to be seen where he was, or anywhere else.

By the time it was daylight, there would be dozens of fat young pheasants struggling in the mouths of the creepways with nylon line round their ankles.

There was nothing to be seen or heard or smelled. Dan wondered how he knew there was another man near him. He supposed there had been a movement too slight for him to have been consciously aware of it, together with a sound too faint for him consciously to have heard it, and a part of his mind, trained beyond his own awareness of it, had put the two side by side and told the rest of his mind what it meant.

Something like that.

Dan waited, straining every sense, looking and listening for confirmation, for any movement. He not only wanted to be sure there was a man, he badly wanted to know what sort of man it was. Until he knew, he could make no plan. Even if he knew, there might be no plan to make.

Though it was still very dark, the covert was beginning to wake up. One of the guardian bantams gave a sleepy, ill-tempered cluck. A starling whistled. There were faint hints of movement in the undergrowth, maybe rabbits or guinea fowl or a hunting cat from a farmyard.

It was stalemate. Dan could not move without the extreme risk of giving himself away, supposing he was not given away already. Giving himself, his position and purpose away might not matter, but it might matter very much. It simply depended who the other was, what he was, what he was doing.

What he was doing at the moment was exactly the same as Dan. Nothing. Probably he couldn't go on like that any longer than Dan could. Probably not as long. But he was managing at the moment.

Was he big, small, young, old, tough, frail, honest, bent, peaceable, violent?

There were, on reflection, two serious possibilities.

One was that Edgar Bland knew that Peggy Bowman knew that he, Edgar Bland, was going to be away for the night; that Peggy was an old girlfriend of Dan's; that Dan would know Edgar Bland was away; that Dan would come to the covert; that Edgar Bland had somehow got hold of a man who could move quietly in the dark; and that that man was now waiting for Dan to pick up the first of his pheasants, so that he could catch him red-handed under the muzzle of a twelve-bore.

30

Yes, that was a serious possibility, and it explained why the man was keeping so utterly still and quiet.

The other possibility—the one Dan had at first favoured—seemed less and less likely with each moment of static stalemate. If the bloke was another poacher, why wasn't he poaching?

Maybe he thought Dan was a keeper. That was funny, but not very, because if he really thought so, and he was a heavy villain from a town, he might kill Dan with his sawn-off shotgun. That would be the weapon he'd have, if he was what he might be.

To a most unusual extent, Dan was baffled and unhappy. He had no idea what to do. For the moment it was right to go on doing nothing, in the hope that the other did something. In the hope that the other, perhaps, began to get frostbite before Dan did. But Dan himself, chilled and cramped and crouched, was beginning to feel the cold creeping in between his ribs, disabling his hands and feet, disabling his brain.

There was no sign of the dawn. There was no breath of wind. The owls had fallen silent. The air was colder and the ground harder. The dead leaves under the edge of the wood were crisped by the frost. They'd crunch like cornflakes.

There was a little more, always a little more, anonymous activity within the covert, as that small crowded world prepared to wake up. There were rustles and sleepy squawks.

There might have been a man on the walkable path in the covert. On the path, if he knew exactly where everything was, he could move in almost total silence.

What man? Another keeper coming for Dan? A third poacher? A second poacher, and the man outside was a keeper waiting for him? A keeper, and the poacher outside was hiding from him? These were all possibilities. Either one or both of the others might know Dan was there. If there was a third. It still might be a cat or a fox or a guinea fowl disturbing the bantams in the trees.

The squawks were not hysterical. The bantams were disturbed but they did not think they were in danger. None of Edgar Bland's booby traps was sprung. Yet the man, if there was a man, must have been on the path, or he would be making far more noise than he was making.

Dan became certain that he had imagined the man on the path. He was still sure, almost wholly illogically, that there was a man in the edge of the wood, but he was now sure that there was nobody inside the wood.

Then he did a turnaround. He became sure that his first idea was right. There was something in the wood, coming very slowly down the path. It had to be the path, because of the silence of his movement. It had to be a man, because no animal would move so slowly. What made Dan sure something was moving in the wood was the movement of the small, irritated response. The clucks were nearer. That wasn't a roosting bantam moving and then clucking again. It was a different bantam. The man was coming to the end of the path and out into the field.

There was a stile at the end of the path. Dan had filled it up below with an armful of dead bracken, because the space was too broad to snare, and a few pheasants might have taken it into their heads to go that way. If there was a man, he was approaching the stile, going as slow as the hour hands of a clock.

Dan, in the edge of the wood, was twelve yards to the north of the stile. The other hiding man was maybe seven yards to the south of the stile. When the man in the wood came to the stile, he would be very roughly halfway between the two of them. So what? Then what? Did the man in the wood sit on the stile, with a twelve-bore on his knees, waiting to bag his poacher at first light?

His two poachers?

The stile was in the thickest of the thick darkness at the edge of the wood. For all his exceptional eyesight, for all his intense concentration, Dan could make out absolutely nothing.

The situation was puzzling, unexpected, and thoroughly dangerous. Dan thought he had better cut away out of it. His movement was almost bound to be detected, in this utterly still and frozen hour before the dawn. But nobody was going to hit him with anything in the dark.

Unless they had a dog, something like a police dog, an Alsatian or Doberman. Was that possible? Could there have been a dog like that, all this time, with the man outside the wood, and Dan not aware of it? Could the other man have come down the path with a big heavy dog?

Dan was sorely tempted to cut and run, but he held still. It was not the thought of a dog that restrained him, because he did not think there was any dog in the wood or outside it. It was the thought of the pheasants he would be leaving behind. He could not bear to think of all those birds caught, and himself far away. The prospect was odious. It was possible that the other two men would in some way cancel each other out, one frightening the other away and then giving chase—something like that. There was no way of knowing if this was more or less likely than any of the other possible outcomes. It was not a chance to bet on. But for the moment there was no need to bet, but only to hold still and hope not to die of cold.

Something was happening at the stile.

There was nothing to be seen, and almost nothing to be heard. But somebody was at the stile, perhaps on it, perhaps over it. Then there was silence. Three of them were risking frostbite. The situation was ludicrous. And dawn was coming.

Suddenly the stalemate was broken, in the way Dan least expected.

A big flashlight was switched on. It was the other man in the edge of the wood. He was a keeper, then, thought Dan dizzily. The beam swung not towards Dan but towards the stile. It lit the startled face of Edgar Bland, who was squatting by the stile with a shotgun.

"Hey!" said Edgar Bland, as surprised as Dan was.

Then the beam of the flashlight swung away from Edgar Bland. It went to the edge of the wood by the stile, and probed along it. Sick, Dan saw it come towards him. It found him. He was skewered on the beam like a bug on a pin.

"Ah," said Edgar Bland. "Dan Mallett, by God. An' we caught ye square."

Edgar Bland had a big flashlight of his own. He turned it on Dan, who felt like a star of the ballet in two spotlights, or a bomber in an old movie in crisscross searchlights.

Dan had to run. He tried to do so. But he was too cold and cramped. There was no sensation in his feet; his legs would not support his weight. He crumpled, swearing softly, helpless until he got his circulation back.

Edgar Bland was crowing with triumph.

"I thank ye, whoever ye be," he said in the direction of the third man.

34

Even in his despair, Dan had time to be puzzled. When the flashlight came on, it was obvious the third man was working with Edgar Bland. Now this was by no means obvious.

The third man's flash remained on Dan. It stayed on him as the man approached. Edgar Bland also approached, holding his shotgun, his flashlight clipped to his belt. Edgar Bland stood over Dan, full in the beam of the third man's light. That too seemed to be clipped to a belt, to leave the man's arms free. Dan wondered numbly who he was, doing Edgar Bland's dirty work for him without Edgar Bland knowing about it. The man remained completely invisible behind the glare of his flashlight.

Edgar Bland stood over Dan, who was trying to rub life back into his legs. He was laughing outright, triumphant, vindictive. Dan didn't blame him. It was a fair cop.

There was an extraordinary noise from behind the third man's flashlight. It was not like anything Dan had ever heard before. It was something between a very powerful metallic twang, and a sharp slap.

There was another noise, simultaneous. It came from above Dan, from Edgar Bland. It came from something which hit Edgar Bland in the neck. The impact was terrific. It knocked him over. When he fell he lay still. He broke his flashlight when he fell.

The third man's flashlight went out, and Dan heard running feet.

He could not have followed. He was not sure he wanted to follow, until he knew what had hit Edgar Bland.

He groped up the motionless body to an arm and to a wrist. There was no pulse.

He groped up to the neck, where the missile had hit.

Out of Edgar Bland's neck was sticking a short metal shaft with feathers at the end. It was an arrow. Edgar Bland had been killed with a crossbow.

And nobody would believe a third man had been there. And Dan had motive as well as opportunity. Resisting arrest. A common and cowardly crime.

Edgar Bland had done more to ruin Dan in death than he'd ever managed in life.

3

DAN SQUATTED on his heels by the body. He tried to think, but it was difficult because of the agonising pins-and-needles of his returning circulation.

The other poacher was armed with a lethal and comparatively silent weapon. He had killed Edgar Bland to evade arrest. No—he was not in imminent danger of arrest. He had killed to prevent Dan's arrest. Why? Did he like Dan?

Or did he hate Dan? That was equally possible, from the bare and peculiar facts of the situation.

Dan had seen crossbows in the window of a gunsmith in Milchester. They were expensive and deadly. You could fit a telescopic sight. The arrows could be bird-bolts, with blunt ends to knock down without lacerating, or tipped with heavy barbed steel points.

When they got into the wrong hands they could do dreadful things to calves and sheep and cats, as well as to deer or straw targets. People said they should be licensed, like shotguns. Dan began to think that the people were right, although he had never bought a licence for gun, dog, radio or anything else.

It would be supposed that Dan had stolen the crossbow, either to shoot game or to shoot a gamekeeper. This assumption would instantly be made by half the village, and by the Chief Detective Superintendent who looked like a fox, and by the Detective Sergeant who looked like a Hereford bullock. They had a point. Nothing in his past made the assumption unlikely, except that he had never shot anybody. A fair number of people would be surprised that he had shot Edgar Bland, but very few people would be completely incredulous.

Why would people guess it was him? Because he was automatically suspected of almost everything, by all the gamekeepers and all the police. And he had had a sort of running battle with Edgar Bland for years. Everybody knew that. It gave him more of a kick to lift birds out of Cobb Wood than any other covert. Everybody knew that, too.

Peggy Bowman had told him Edgar Bland was going to be away. Would the police know that? They'd find out that Peggy knew, probably, from Major March. They might find out that Peggy was an old flame of Dan's, and still a friend of his. They'd ask her if she'd told anybody. She'd surely deny telling anybody, for her own sake as well as for Dan's. How many other people would have known, or would have thought they knew, that Edgar Bland was going away? Major March himself. Maybe one or two others, in the household or on the estate. And Edgar's wife. Would any of them tell anybody? Why would they?

Dan could be connected to the murder by history and by his own reputation. But he couldn't be convicted by those, not if there was no other evidence. At least, he thought not. But there was more against him, much more, if the police found out about the conversation in the pigeon loft. And if they found the snares, the thirty-eight artistically laid snares.

Dan wanted to run away now, and hide in his bed, and say he'd never left it. His mother would give him an alibi. Nobody would believe it, but she'd stand firm if she was cross-examined by the Lord Chancellor. From every point of view except one, running away now was infinitely the best thing to do. But now that the snares were set, nothing was going to stop dozens of pheasants walking into them, and presently advertising the fact with a lot of indignant noise.

Dan sighed. He rose and stretched painfully. He still badly wanted a lot of pheasants, to add to the hip-operation fund. But this was not the night to get them. Little as he'd liked Edgar Bland, he couldn't go poaching pheasants round his dead body. That would be downright unseemly. Besides, if he was by any small chance seen near the covert in the dawn, or seen with birds, and Edgar Bland's body was found . . .

Dan sighed, and went to the corner of the wood, and began to crawl up the length of the edge of the wood picking up his snares.

He did not think anyone would notice the changes he had made to the mouths of the creepways. Edgar Bland would have noticed, all right, and done the right sums in his head.

He collected the snares, with fingers again numbed almost to uselessness, and wound them onto their cards. As he did so, he found himself considering another aspect of the situation.

Peggy Bowman had been quite sure Edgar Bland was

39

going to the nursing home. That was in the late afternoon. Somebody changed the arrangement, unknown to her, probably after she got off work and went home to George and the telly. Major March told Edgar Bland to cancel his trip and guard his covert. But, according to Peggy, Major March had already given him permission to go. All the same, it must have been something like that. But why?

It was as though somebody had tipped somebody off that Dan was going to Cobb Wood. But that could only be Peggy, and it couldn't possibly be Peggy. Had someone overheard the conversation in the pigeon loft? It was possible in theory, and it explained everything, but it was terribly unlikely. Who would hide in a pigeon loft to eavesdrop? Nobody could have known Dan was going there. He only did go there because he was running short of maize, and it was convenient from Sir George Simpson's.

Dan pictured somebody after Peggy, fancying her, hiding in the pigeon loft to jump out at her. That was possible. She was still very attractive, though she had grown thicker than Dan liked. But a pigeon loft was a rotten place for that sort of thing, all those birds flapping and pecking round you. Maybe Peggy had had an assignation with a boyfriend. Anybody married to George would be apt to have a boyfriend. And Dan had interrupted them, and the boyfriend had hidden in the pen room. That was possible, too. Dan had hidden in much odder places, and heard some pretty funny things while hiding. But Peggy hadn't been like a girl interrupted in the act, or just before the act, or just after it. She'd been glad to see him, bored and glad of a diversion. So it had seemed to Dan, and he did not think he could be wrong about that.

Dan thought there was something very funny and fishy

40

about all this. He was extremely angry that his night's work had been scuppered. He was sorry about Edgar Bland and a good deal shocked by the murder.

Something had changed Edgar Bland's mind or Major March's mind, enough to cancel the arrangements Edgar Bland had made and the permission Major March had given. A tip-off. That was infinitely the most likely.

Maybe not about Dan at all, about something quite different. Maybe about a villain from a town, a man with an expensive crossbow, a man who had said something incautious in a back-street Milchester pub . . .

This suddenly seemed very much more likely. It was a line of thought that might even establish who the villain was. At least what sort of bloke he was, what he was after, where he was from. All this was information Dan wanted very badly indeed. It would make a large difference to him—about twenty years' difference. A large difference to his dogs and his birds and his mother.

Almost certainly it was no good asking Peggy Bowman about the tip-off, because almost certainly she knew nothing about it. If she'd heard, early the previous evening, she'd have sent Dan a warning somehow. She was a good enough friend for that.

It was no good asking Major March. The very thought of that conversation almost made Dan laugh, though he felt very far from laughter.

The person to ask, the obvious and only person, was Edgar Bland's wife. Surely she'd know, something if not everything. She must do, expecting the old bastard—Dan checked himself, shocked—expecting the poor bloke to be away and then finding him home and guarding his covert.

She'd be up pretty soon, getting Edgar's breakfast.

41

He'd want a lot of it, after a night of watching in the frost.

It seemed a morbid, a cynical thing to do, to go and ask a woman such questions when her man was lying half a mile away with an arrow in his neck. But it would be no help to Beryl Bland, or to Edgar either, to have Dan sent up for something he didn't do.

Dan wondered about hiding the body. There didn't seem much point. People knew where Edgar Bland had been going. When he didn't turn up later, they'd search for him. Dan couldn't hide him so that they couldn't find him, in the river or anywhere else. And if he was seen trying, he was for it for certain.

Dan went round the wood, crossed the stream by the footbridge, and sat under a hedge near the Blands' cottage. It was terribly cold. He waited for signs of life.

A lot of people who knew the stories would have been surprised to see him come knocking on the Blands' door, even if Edgar wasn't there. They'd expect Beryl to slam the door in his face, at the first sight of him, especially after the business of the brace of partridges. But things weren't quite like that. The reason was shocking, really. Dan's father had been a man of Dan's own build and appearance, with the same sort of eyes and the same sort of smile and the same taste for girls. Dan's mother had loved him all her life, in spite of his wicked ways—she couldn't help herself. A lot of other girls couldn't help themselves, either, and one of them was Beryl Bland.

It was not certain if Edgar Bland ever knew this. If he did, his hatred of Dan's father maybe explained part of his hatred of Dan.

The result was that Beryl had a soft spot for Dan—he reminded her so strongly of his Dad. She admitted this to him, quite freely, with a giggle like a young girl's, though she'd never have breathed a word to anybody else. Edgar Bland was a hard, unforgiving man.

Waiting in the bitter cold, Dan wondered if this was a sensible way to be spending his time. He thought on balance that it was, but it was certainly unpleasant. He stamped and swung his arms, and finished the whisky in his flask.

The sky began to pale in the east, a very cold, clear, yellowish pallor, beautiful but cruel. The stars disappeared. Some birds chirruped unconvincingly. Beryl would soon be up and about, as his own mother would have been in the days of her strength.

Dan saw a light go on in the upstairs window of the cottage, then in a downstairs window. In the still, freezing air he heard a door open and close. A dog was being let out or a cat in. Dan waited for smoke from the chimney.

The sky was bright when Dan walked up the garden path, between the sad frozen remnants of Beryl's little borders. He had never been here before. In spite of Beryl's soft spot, it was not—had not been—a good place for him to be. The cottage was new and ugly. There were two panes of frosted glass in the door, and between them a bell push.

Dan pressed the bell. An inch away from his finger, through the thin pane of the door, came a melodious ding-dong.

Dan thought an electric bell that went ding-dong was one of the silliest ways to spend money he ever heard of.

"Forget your latch-key, did ye?" called Beryl's voice from inside. "Okay, I'm comin'."

She opened the door, through which came a strong and

43

delicious smell of frying bacon. Dan's heart gave a little jump, between pity and misery and fright. Beryl was frying that bacon for Edgar. Edgar by now would have white frost in his hair.

Beryl had put on plenty of weight, since the days thirty years before when she met Dan's father in the old watermill. Her face had become jowly and coarse in texture, with lines of dissatisfaction round her mouth. Her hair was pepper-and-salt, now contorted into plastic rollers. She was wearing a greasy satin dressing gown, and fluffy mules over which a lot of breakfast bacon, over the years, had spat its fat.

She looked at Dan with utter stupefaction.

"Ye better get away out o' this quick," she said. "'E'll be back any mennit."

"Nay," said Dan, trying to talk exactly as his father had talked. "Your man went off in a motorcar."

"'E never! Wi' who?"

"I dunno. Bloke wi' a long white face."

"What were ye doen t'Cobb Wood?"

"'Aven me night's work wasted," said Dan, grinning his widest and most innocent grin.

Beryl smiled back at him. She had tried to frown, but the smile seemed to take her by surprise.

Dan hated to cheat this decent woman who liked him. As he followed her into the cottage kitchen, he was on the verge of telling her exactly what had happened. It was her right to know.

But she would go clamorously to pieces, and he would get no sense out of her. Feeling cold-hearted and cruel, he knew he must keep her in her fool's paradise until she had told him what she knew. When her screams permitted, she would either insist on being taken at once to the body, or else ring up the police.

"How's yer Ma?" asked Beryl, giving Dan a cup of strong tea.

"Not so spry."

"Poor soul. But there's a 'oman I always did envy."

They chatted amicably, safe from interruption. Beryl accepted that Edgar had gone off in a car with a stranger, having ruined Dan's night's work for him.

"That were a puzzle," said Dan. "I 'eard confidential 'e were off t'Quimbury."

"Ye of all men shouldn't of 'eard that, Dan Mallett."

"Shocken breach o' trust," agreed Dan, with another of his largest grins. "It were a nasty shock finden 'im lurken wi' a cannon."

"Yer, well, they phoned from the nursin' 'ome, sayen'e weren't t'come. A doctor were maken a special visit or summat. Then there were a call from the Major, tellen Ed t'go to the wood."

"From the Major 'imself?"

"No, I b'lieve it were a message. A secketerry or a servan', I dunno. Ed answered it. I was cooken 'is lordship's supper. Right fussy 'e's got."

"Ah," said Dan, trying to hide his intense interest. "Any special reason the Major give?"

Beryl giggled, the pretty young girl once again peeping out of the plump, tired woman.

"Message said," she told Dan, "a special dreadful rogue was a-goen t'the wood."

"Go on," said Dan with difficulty.

"You, m'dear. Ed was out arter you."

Dan's favourite theory collapsed.

And he had admitted to Beryl that he'd been in Cobb Wood. He'd had to, in order to ask his question. It was perhaps a great mistake. Maybe it showed he was more tired than he thought, or rattled by a murder taking place a few inches from his face.

Meanwhile it was time he got away home, before the countryside was full of inquisitive people, and before his mother started worrying. Beryl was also beginning to get anxious, in case Edgar came back from his business in the car.

Dan felt a keen and unusual stab of conscience, grinning at Beryl and drinking her tea.

He glanced through the open door of the sitting room, as they passed it on the way to the front door.

"Gum," he said, at the sight of the new carpet, the enormous television set, the terrible cocktail cabinet, the fancy modernistic clock.

"The Major ben generous wi' bonuses," said Beryl. "God knows why."

"'Ope ye saved some," said Dan.

"'Ope so too," said Beryl. "Ed's getten near retirement."

She opened the door cautiously and peeped out.

"No signs," she said. "Ta for callen. It's nice to 'ave a laugh. It do make a change from a bloke wi' a lemon in 'is mouth."

Dan thanked her, grinned, and slipped away. He thought it was a sickening irony that Berly should be watching out to save him, Dan, from an embarrassing meeting with her husband. And that she should have made those unthinking, frivolous remarks about a man of whom, had she known what Dan ought to have told her, she would have spoken with tearful loyalty.

He went home quickly, but not by a route an ordinary man would have chosen. Its advantage was that no one saw him.

He tried to think as he went.

Major March had rung up Edgar Bland, or caused him to be rung up, with news about Dan. The source could only have been Peggy. This remained entirely incredible, but it now had to be faced. Dan had been fairly stealthy, approaching and leaving the pigeon loft, but he had not taken exaggerated precautions. There had seemed no need to crawl like a centipede into the place. It was not so very dreadful to chat to an old friend, and the bag of maize could have been a loan to a fellow fancier. Maybe he was seen. Maybe whoever saw him knew about him and Peggy in the old days, or told someone who did. Then perhaps Major March called for Peggy, grilled her, threatened her, got it out of her, then stopped her getting a warning to Dan.

Dan was worried for Peggy. He was very worried for himself. Major March and others, as well as Peggy, knew he was going to Cobb Wood.

Perhaps after all it hardly mattered that he told Beryl he'd been there.

His body was warm with Beryl's boot-polish tea and with his own rapid journey. But there was a chilly finger of alarm probing at his guts.

47

Dan went by Medwell Priory and through the Priory Woods, approaching his own cottage invisibly. Far away he heard the first cars.

He heard a police car. He thought it was in Poulter's Lane. It might be going to the Blands' cottage or it might be going to Cobb Wood.

Dan wondered about giving himself up and telling the exact truth. The idea was no sooner born than it was dead. The police would simply wonder where he'd hidden his crossbow.

What, then? He needed to know more about the tip-off, the events of the previous evening. He needed to talk to people, to Peggy Bowman above all and then to others. He had to do that without being seen by anybody. But you can't talk to people without them seeing you, unless you use the telephone. What telephone? The call box outside the general stores in the village, glass walls on three sides, so you stood like a goldfish in a bowl?

Dan tried as he prowled through the wood to make sense of what had happened.

Amongst all the oddities, there was an oddity about the nursing home. Surely it was peculiar to visit an elderly, confused, bedridden patient in the evening. Surely it was peculiar to ring up and cancel an appointment. Because of a visit from a doctor, Beryl had said—something like that. Surely that was peculiar, too.

Trying to make bricks with no straw whatever, Dan examined all this. Suppose Edgar Bland had invented the evening appointment, as an excuse to go and spend a night with his married daughter. Would he do that? He could see her whenever he liked, his own daughter, only over there in Quimbury, a matter of twelve miles. Well then, for some other reason. A girl. Edgar Bland with a girl? Was that possible? At his age? With his miserable personality? If there was no appointment, there was no cancellation. Edgar Bland had made that up, to Beryl and anyone else involved. Why? Because it wasn't the nursing home ringing up, it was the girl, saying her husband had come home. And her husband was the bloke with the crossbow. Not a poacher at all.

Well, that was all possible—that or something on those lines. There was a way of checking up on it, part of, testing part of the theory. Talk to the nursing home.

Dan searched in his memory. He did not think either Beryl or Peggy had mentioned the name of the nursing home. He had not asked, because he had not then wanted to know. He did not think either woman had mentioned the name of the old man Edgar Bland visited. Were there many nursing homes near Quimbury? How near? The post office in Quimbury would know; so presumably would a local doctor. Did nursing homes advertise in the yellow pages?

Dan concluded that he had to go to Quimbury. He had to go not as a poacher or an odd-job man, but as a bank manager. He had to change his clothes. He was passionately hungry. It was unfeeling to be hungry with Edgar Bland dead and Beryl, by now, sobbing hysterically, but there the fact was. He needed his morning nap, too—it was coming up time for it. He needed a car. Not Fred Dawson's old red Ford van, but a bank manager's car.

The sun rose, and strengthened, and began to melt the hoarfrost where it struck. It was a morning of great beauty. Three bullfinches were busy about something at the edge of the wood, two brilliant gentlemen and a sad grey lady. Far above them, in the tops of the trees, was a small flock of early fieldfares, come to England for the winter from their breeding grounds far inside the Arctic Circle. They were nervous of Dan; they did not see such creatures in Lapland or far-northern Russia. Soon, feeling more at home, they would be feeding on the ground in big mixed flocks of a dozen species. Dan took small pleasure in watching them. He wanted his breakfast and the nap he was not going to get, and he wanted knowledge. Without it he was near enough dead and his mother was near enough dead.

4

As always, Dan washed and shaved in the kitchen, while sausages sizzled in a pan on the range. He shaved carefully. Today was not a day for being a poacher, but for being something quite different. He went upstairs and dressed accordingly, in a white shirt with a semistiff collar, a dark blue suit—old, but carefully preserved—and a soberly patterned tie. He put on the neat black shoes which he particularly hated.

When he left after breakfast he carried away with him, guiltily as ever, the memory of his mother's grimly and tragically disapproving face. It was the clothes that did it: the reminder of the long-gone days of hope, of the cherished might-have-been.

Dan went delicately through the woods, to safeguard his aging bank-manager's suit and his neat little black shoes. He went to the rabbit hole which he called his Current Account—small sums, for day-to-day needs—as against the deeper and more obscure burrow which he called his Deposit Account. He filled a pocket with silver and copper, and took a few pounds of paper money.

What he needed was a car. Most of the village would be wide awake by now, and much of it already on the way to

51

its various jobs. Car stealing had become difficult. But twelve miles was too far to walk.

His first idea was to go for some classless, anonymous, mass-produced kind of car, a Ford or Morris or one of the smaller Japanese types. Then he considered the impression he wanted to make: the impact of his arrival, the chance of getting answers to his questions. He went to Medwell Court, and slid under the wheel of Major March's Mercedes.

He had thought to take Major March's second car, the Peugeot, which lived in the country, not this great gleaming bus which he drove down from London. He had thought Major March was away, from finding Peggy Bowman in the dovecote and from what Peggy said. He generally kept pretty good track of the movements of the local mobs, keeping at all times an eye on the main chance. This time he was caught out. But he still kept the eye on the main chance, and the Mercedes was the morning's chance.

He had never driven such a powerful car before. He quite enjoyed it. He seemed to get to Quimbury in about eleven seconds.

Quimbury was a large, charmless village with one outstanding charm: nobody there knew Dan. At least, nobody there had ever seen him dressed as he was dressed today. He parked the Mercedes behind a pub, and walked to the post office. He walked with a sort of squirarchic swagger copied from Major March, who had himself copied it, Dan supposed, from performances on films of bluff old English squires.

The post office, as Dan expected, had a classified directory inside and a public telephone box outside.

Six nursing homes were listed in the immediate area. Half a dozen others, a little more remote, were possible.

Dan cursed himself for not knowing the name of the nursing home which Edgar Bland visited, or that of the man he visited. He did not even know the name of the Blands' married daughter.

He began telephoning nursing homes from the call box. He felt like a goldfish in a bowl in the glass-sided box, but he did not think anybody who knew him would walk down the village street of Quimbury. He blessed the foresight that had made him fill his trouser pocket with copper and silver, though he cursed his lack of foresight in other directions.

He spoke to each nursing home in his bank manager's voice. He said he was Captain Cavendish. He said he was a friend of Major March, of Medwell Court. None of the nursing homes had heard of Major March. He said that Major March had a keeper who visited, semiregularly, an elderly ex-employer, and spoke in glowing terms of the home he visited. Captain Cavendish was himself looking for a suitable nursing home for his aunt. Major March's gamekeeper had warmly (though respectfully) recommended the home where his ex-employer lay. This was just the other day, when Captain Cavendish was shooting Major March's partridges, and the subject had come up while they were having their picnic by the Land Rover.

Captain Cavendish thought the nursing home he was talking to was the one to which Major March's gamekeeper had referred. In five successive cases it was not.

In the sixth case it was. It was the Rosebank Nursing Home, described in the yellow pages as fully registered and approved, with resident S.R.N., single and shared rooms, day and night nursing, for long or short stays, convalescence, elderly patients, sunny lounge with colour television, visits by appointment only.

Dan had actually tried the Rosebank second, to meet only an answering machine. He had not felt like telling his wearying rigmarole to a cassette, so he tried three others before he returned to it. A curious person answered: it might have been a man with a high voice or a woman with a low voice. He began his story. He was transferred almost at once, very politely, to "Matron." Matron did not speak, but fluted, or twittered. She sounded sweet but pretty silly. She said at once that they knew Mr. Bland, that he had indeed come monthly to visit dear old Colonel Forbes, that it was very good of him to come, that Colonel Forbes quite looked forward to the visits, and was quite perky when Mr. Bland came, and that the poor old gentleman had scarcely any other visitors, since his family, such as they were, were all in Scotland or abroad.

Dan described the predicament of his aunt. He described his mother—the arthritis, the inability to look after herself. He added a note of confusion, of senility, which would have filled his mother with justified rage if she had heard it.

Matron said that there was no vacancy at Rosebank, just at the moment, for a long-stay patient who needed supervision. But at any moment there might be.

"Many of our resident patients are very elderly, Captain Cavendish," said Matron, "and vacancies do—if you understand me—quite suddenly occur!"

Dan thought he understood about the Rosebank. It was a place where families who couldn't be bothered, and who could afford it, put their aunts to die.

Which might often be a good thing, a necessary thing. The Matron he was talking to certainly sounded kind.

"I quite understand your position," he said bluffly to the telephone. "In my poor aunt's case there is, ah, urgency, but not pressing urgency, if I make myself clear."

It seemed he made himself clear. It seemed that urgency, but not pressing urgency, was the case with most of the Rosebank's patients.

On this basis he made an appointment to visit the Rosebank at half-past three in the afternoon. He could see the garden, the lounge, one or two of the rooms; he could meet Matron herself and some of her devoted staff.

"It is *rather* difficult to find," said Matron. "We are *quite* secluded—so very quiet, you know—a healing atmosphere of rural calm!"

Dan said he liked rural calm.

Matron began to give him directions, but became almost at once herself hopelessly confused.

"Oh, silly me!" she fluted. "What will you think of us?"

She handed Dan over to the other voice, high man or low woman, who in a gentle local accent gave Dan clear and competent directions. Evidently it was something that had to be done often. The place sounded secluded indeed. Dan wondered if the Mercedes would get over the little bridges and down the tiny lanes the voice described.

It did, but only just.

Rosebank was evidently converted, though it was difficult to say from what. The central part was a modest mock-Tudor house, built perhaps in 1930, with whitewashed walls between tacked-on beams. There was a single-story wing in greyish pebble dash, quite new, sticking out at one side, with a depressing clinical look; and another, newer, of cheaper materials, on the other side, which looked like a bit of a modern primary school. There was no telling from the outside if the place was good or bad, kindly or cynical.

There was a big, untidy garden round the place. On two sides of the garden there were woods, and on the third side a scrubby mixed hedge through which could be seen grassland falling away towards a little river.

Dan pressed a bell marked "Visitors." He had not the remotest idea what to expect. He had never been inside a nursing home. Meanwhile he assumed the air of serious confidence which had served him well in the bank, and sometimes since, when he acted parts like today's part.

He waited for a long time. He pressed the bell again. He heard it ring a long way away, unlike Beryl Bland's ding-dong which was stuck to the inside of the door. The place was utterly silent. There was no sign of life. Dan wondered if they were all dead, staff as well as patients.

The door opened, but only five inches. It was held by a heavy brass chain. A small black face peeped out, under a very clean white cap. It was a young nurse, a very pretty girl.

"Matron is expecting me," said Dan.

"Your name, please?" said the nurse, in a voice that sounded at least as educated as Dan's bank-manager voice.

Dan had a panic-stricken moment of blankness. What was his name?

"Mr. Cavendish," he said, after a long moment that must have made him look extremely stupid. "Captain Cavendish," he corrected himself.

56

Yes, he was expected. The little nurse smiled and nodded, and unchained the door. When she opened the door Dan was able to see her properly. She was worth a second look and a third. On a miniature scale her figure was marvellous, tiny-waisted, doing lovely things back and front to the trim white nurse's uniform. Her smile was broad—not a smile but a grin. Dan smiled back, responding to the simple, infectious friendliness in the girl's face. He made no attempt to hide the admiration he was feeling. He had always taken the view that, when you admired a pretty girl, you might as well show it.

She said, "This way, please. I'll tell Matron you're here."

He followed her down a long, dark hall. He wanted to inspect these surroundings that were so strange to him: he also wanted to inspect the nurse. She moved well, at once gracefully and bouncily, like a dancer. The active little black body could with delightful ease be imagined under the cool, starched white cotton. Dan called himself to attention, and looked at the doors they were passing. On each was a little slot with a card; on each card a name written. Dan saw Colonel Forbes, Mrs. Metcalfe, Miss Nickson, Mr. Plante. Behind each door he imagined some ancient, feeble, yellowish, apathetic victim of the years and of a hard-faced family.

He returned to contemplation of the little nurse's behind, bouncing cheerfully under her cotton skirt in front of him.

She opened a door into a small, bright, chintzy room. There were two or three chairs, a writing table covered in papers, a telephone and intercom, a filing cabinet. It was an office, but without the depressing air of an office which, years before, had nearly driven Dan out of his mind. There were several small oils on the walls, land-scapes, amateur but pleasant; a big bowl of fresh flowers, which, in October, must have cost a fortune at a florist; bright floral curtains and a bright Indian rug.

Dan wanted to detain his guide, but she went away to find Matron, who was evidently a local god.

She was not like a god, but like somebody's favourite aunt. She was another little woman, with untidy pepper-and-salt hair. Dan thought she was in her late fifties. She had the expression of someone who was trying to remember what she had to do next, but knew that it would be highly enjoyable when she did it. She was dressed not in uniform but in a tweed coat and skirt. She wore a wedding ring. Her shoes were expensive.

She shook hands with Dan, and apologised for keeping him waiting. In the flesh she was as twittery and fluting as she had sounded on the telephone. She had forgotten why Dan had come, but her smile and her twinkling grey eyes said that she was enchanted to see him.

"I do feel such a goose," she said, "but *just* after your call this morning dear old Mr. Plante was found halfway up the ladder to the attic! None of us could imagine how he got so far! Nurse had taken her eyes off him just for a second, you know, and he was off like a monkey! We had an awful job getting him down off the ladder! But one couldn't be cross, you know. It's so wonderful when they show a bit of spirit! What can be depressing about this work is when they just sit in lonely misery, looking in-wards. . . . We're not as grand as some of the homes. But what we try above all to do is to give some *time* to the patients. They want someone to talk to! No more than that! And then they get a little tired, and off they go to sleep."

"If they sleep a lot in the day," suggested Dan diffidently, "don't they get wakeful in the night?"

"Indeed they do, Colonel Cavenham—have I got that quite right?"

"Captain Cavendish," said Dan, thinking quickly.

"What will you think of me? From one moment to the next . . . ! Luckily each patient's medication is written down, or the dear lord knows what I'd dose them with! Yes, in answer to your question, the dear old things do wake up in the night, and often they want to talk! Dear Mrs. Metcalfe only ever wants to talk in the middle of the night! About Egypt, usually. . . . Such a good thing. How bored the night-duty Sisters would be, with everybody in the house fast asleep!"

Matron showed Dan the rooms of Miss Nickson and Mr. Plante. The former was out for a drive with her great-niece; the latter, weaned for the moment from ladders, was in the lounge watching a children's programme on the television. The rooms were all right. They did not look like hospital rooms, except for plastic vessels under the beds of depressing shape, and pieces of sinister tubing, and a certain bleakness. There were no books, newspapers, pictures or radios.

"They lose interest in the outside world," said Matron. "It is often very difficult for visitors to know what to talk to them about!"

This remark enabled Dan to slide into the conversation the name of Edgar Bland.

Matron looked completely blank. Nudged, she remembered perfectly. It was dear old Colonel Forbes that Mr.

Bland visited. They were not *very* rewarding visits, as the poor old Colonel was confused, after his second stroke, and mistook poor Mr. Bland for ever so many different people. But it was kind of Mr. Bland to come. He was laying up treasure in heaven.

"On earth too, perhaps," said Dan mildly.

Matron understood perfectly. Her laugh was a little shocked.

"Oh no, Captain er," she said. "Like many of our patients, Colonel Forbes' affairs are all in the hands of the lawyers. We send them the bills, and forward all correspondence. There is no question of his writing out a cheque, or changing his will, or anything of that sort."

"Ah," said Dan, wondering if Edgar Bland had known this. "I believe," he said, "speaking of Bland, that he was coming here yesterday evening?"

"We expected him, yes," said Matron. "He telephoned, asking especially if he might make an evening appointment. We do have to insist, you know, that all visits are made by appointment. Because doctors come and doctors go, and treatments and baths and meals, and we'd all be even more muddled than we are!"

"An evening appointment can't be usual?" hazarded Dan.

"No! Indeed not! Our old people keep *very* early hours! But we could make an exception. Colonel Forbes scarcely knows, you see, whether it's day or night! Time means nothing to him! He was ringing for his breakfast, the night before last, at ten o'clock in the evening! So we gave it to him! A nice boiled egg! Why not? It's so nice to see them eating. However, Mr. Bland did not come. We thought it a little inconsiderate. Nurse waited up specially, you

60

know, because when Colonel Forbes has a visitor he likes to offer them a drink. We give them Bovril. . . . And here is our lounge, and there is Mr. Plante, watching the television."

The lounge was terribly depressing. It was a large, bare room, with chairs of various kinds lining the walls. In some of the chairs old people sat. Some were asleep. Some were staring vacantly at nothing. None was doing anything, anything at all. There were three or four men, half a dozen women. Dan did not ask which Mr. Plante was, the sportive climber of ladders. It was difficult to believe that any of the ancient wrecks of men in the lounge could manage one rung of a ladder.

One of the old men looked up. He saw Matron. His eyes turned outwards instead of inwards. He almost smiled.

He said in a slurred but comprehensible voice, "Veronica, come and sit beside me. There is a programme coming on I want you to watch."

"Later, dear, if I possibly can," said Matron.

She took Dan back to her office, to take particulars of his aunt. There would almost certainly be a room free in a month or six weeks: Colonel Forbes', or some other.

On the way down the hall, they passed a big, soft man pushing a trolley. He was dressed in white; his face and hands were as white as his uniform. Dan averted his eyes from the objects on the trolley, not because he recognized them but because he was afraid of recognizing them.

"Stephen, our orderly," said Matron. "He is supposed to look after the patients, but he looks after everything! The boiler! The painting and decorating! He carries all the luggage, and moves all the furniture!"

Dan shook hands with Stephen, whose hand was dry but flabby. He did not look like a man who stoked boilers or carried luggage.

Stephen said to Matron, "Colonel Forbes is feeling lonely."

"Dear old boy," said Matron. "Of course he is. Especially as he was expecting Mr. Bland yesterday evening." To Dan she said, "Excuse me just a sec, Captain er."

She opened the door which bore Colonel Forbes' name on the card. Dan glimpsed a yellowish face on pillows.

"Oh, there you are, Veronica," said an exhausted, ancient voice. "I need you."

"I know dear," said Matron. In her voice there was nothing but affection. She was neither impatient nor patronising. "I'll be with you just as soon as I've done one or two little jobs, and then we can have a nice talk."

She was not humouring the old man. She was making him a promise Dan was sure she would keep.

Turning back to Dan, Matron said, "Some of the old gentlemen confuse me with their late wives, you know. Colonel Forbes does, and naughty Mr. Plante, whom you saw watching the television. They want to hold my hand, and talk about the old days! I take it as quite a compliment! Of course I let them. If you can't give comfort one way, you can very often find another way."

Stephen said in the high, womanish voice which had given Dan directions. "Poor old Mrs. Parker had another accident with her tea."

"Oh dear! She will insist on pouring it out herself!"

"But I've cleaned it up. No harm done."

"Oh thank you, Stephen. Bless you!"

Stephen gave a mild smile, blinked his mild eyes, and pushed the trolley away.

"The forms, the forms, we must fill in the forms," murmured Matron, pawing a moment later through the drifts of papers on her desk. "Oh! Silly me! I remember I took them upstairs! But I can't remember why! Excuse me just a sec, Colonel er, and I'll run upstairs like a rabbit."

Dan smiled at her retreating back. He thought she was a thoroughly nice woman, probably making money but also motivated by real humanity. The old people he had seen could hardly be described as happy, but they were being treated, he thought, with all possible kindness. Dan had read about "caring" people. Matron was a caring person.

From behind another door Dan heard another old man call, "Veronica!" Matron stopped, glanced back over her shoulder with an expression of comic resignation, looked into the room, and said something comforting. She was standing in for another dead wife.

The nursing home had not rung up to cancel Edgar Bland's appointment. Someone else had, someone who knew he was going there and when. Why? To get him to Cobb Wood instead? To get him there to be killed? Why?

From the window of the office Dan could see the wing of the Mercedes, parked unobtrusively almost out of sight of the road. He decided to leave it at the edge of Quimbury, and take some other vehicle—where?

To Medwell Court. To Peggy Bowman. He had to see Peggy. He had to know more about those increasingly baffling telephone calls. This visit had been necessary, though all that he had learned was negative. That visit was necessary, too, though the thought of it made the hair bristle on the back of his neck.

As he watched, a uniformed policeman crossed the gravel in front of the house, heading for the Mercedes.

He checked the number from a notebook. He turned to call. A police car followed him in.

The car could only be the one Dan had come in. He could not pretend otherwise. There was no other car outside and no other visitor inside.

A police sergeant got out of the police car, and walked towards the front door of Rosebank.

5

OBVIOUSLY Dan must leave, extremely quickly, by some other door than the front door. He remembered that there were doors in each of the new wings. Both were in full view of the sergeant by the front door. There must be a back door in a house of this size. He would slip out of the back door, and hide in the nearby woods. He could get clean away, and borrow another car to go back to Medwell.

Even as he made this easiest of decisions, he saw the first policeman running across the gravel towards a corner of the building. He was going round the back.

The police car backed so that it blocked the gateway out into the road. The driver got out and went to the Mercedes. He turned to face the house. From where he stood he could see the windows of Matron's office. Dan had already undone the catch, preparing to climb out. He did it up again.

He heard the front-door bell from along the passage.

He opened the door of the office a crack, and peeped up and down the passage. The whole building was as quiet as a tomb. The patients made no noise and the staff very little. Nobody had yet appeared to answer the front-door bell. Dan saw the foot of a flight of stairs. In a moment Matron would be coming down them, with the forms for him to fill in. A house like this probably had back stairs. They probably rose from a passage by the kitchen and back premises. They would not be difficult to find, but they would be very difficult to find without being seen.

Dan decided to risk the front stairs, on the basis that Matron would have difficulty finding anything she was looking for.

Dan slipped across the passage, his shoes squeaking on the rubbery material that covered the floor. He went quickly but carefully up the stairs. The stairs were uncarpeted, and creaked deafeningly. There was still no sound or sign of movement.

He paused on a landing. Footsteps were going down the hall on the way to the front door.

He went on up to the next floor. There was another broad passage, better lit than the one downstairs. Half a dozen doors opened off it. Each had a card in a little brass holder, with the name of the inmate written on the card. A second flight of stairs rose. It was full in view of anyone in the passage: but there was no one in the passage.

With his chin on his shoulder, Dan went softly over worn linoleum to the upper staircase. A door opened behind him. Dan saw a glimpse of tweed skirt. Matron. He had no time to get up the stairs. Hoping very hard, he bolted through the nearest door, which was marked "Mrs. Parker." He remembered that Mrs. Parker had had an accident with her tea. Perhaps, cleaned up and comforted, she was now watching the children's television.

He closed the door so that it made no click, and immediately heard Matron's expensive shoes on the linoleum outside. They rattled down the stairs. He heard voices from the hall.

He turned to look at what he hoped was an empty room. A tiny, shrivelled lady in a fawn dressing gown was sitting on a peculiar chair, in a peculiar position. With excruciating embarrassment, Dan realised it was a commode. He wished he had chosen any other room in the building. But he had been given no choice.

He said, in a voice like that of Doctor Smith in Medwell, "And how are we today, Mrs. Parker?"

Mrs. Parker stared unblinkingly in his general direction. With a renewed shock, with a wave of compassion, Dan saw that she was blind.

In a voice of surprising strength she said, "Is that you, Cedric? It is high time you did come to see me, you naughty boy."

"Yes, it's me," said Dan.

He smiled his most winning smile, then abandoned it, remembering that on Mrs. Parker it was wasted.

"I hope you brought your Auntie some money, as I asked," said Mrs. Parker. "I want you to telephone for a taxi to take me home."

Her voice was astonishingly strong. She was fairly bellowing. Any second, somebody was going to come in to see what she was shouting about.

Asylum was no asylum. Dan opened the door a crack, peeped out, and hared away up the second flight of stairs. The passage at the top was narrower, and L-shaped. There were several doors without names on them. A door at the end opened—a door directly above the one Matron had opened. Dan slid round the corner by the top of the stairs. Quick, light footsteps approached. Dan flattened himself against the wall. It seemed likely, but it was a long way from certain, that the person would go down the stairs instead of turning the corner and continuing along the passage.

The person went down the stairs. Dan glimpsed a back. It was a girl. It was the little black nurse.

Did she share a bedroom, or did she have one to herself? If the latter, it was empty just now. Even if the former, it was probably empty in the middle of the afternoon.

Dan tiptoed along the passage to the door the black girl had come out of. She had left it ajar. He peeped in. It was a tiny, bright room, no bigger than his own bedroom in the cottage. It was quite warm. It was full of the bright October afternoon sunshine. It had been a maid's room, but that maid had been a lucky maid to have such a sunny room. If, Dan reflected, maids in a house like this ever got to enjoy the sunshine in their bedrooms.

He shut the door softly behind him. Now what? The police would search the house—they must do. They would keep watch on the outside of the house while they did so. As there were three of them they could arrange that. In any part of the house, Dan would be as visible as an elephant even if he were as small as a beetle.

The room had a wardrobe. If it was stuffed with clothes. . . . Dan opened it. It seemed the little black girl had practically no clothes. A pair of jeans and two checked shirts hung in the wardrobe. There was also a red plastic mackintosh on a book inside the door. Under the bed was no good. The bed was a small, old-fashioned iron one, high, with a skimpy cotton coverlet that barely covered the mattress.

Dan went to the window. There were certain to be downpipes from the gutters, but not necessarily one he could reach. There was one he could reach. It went straight down, then at an angle, and then joined another in a big wrought-iron hopper. Dan, who could climb like a cat, would not have the slightest difficulty climbing down the drain-pipe, assuming it was firmly bolted to the wall: except that a policeman stood at the bottom.

Dan leaned out of the window and looked upwards, trying at the same time to keep an eye on the policeman. The gutter was only a yard above the top of the window. He could get up onto the roof, and come down after dark. It was not at all an attractive prospect, but it was better than any conceivable alternative. The policeman below might perfectly well not look up: though it was true that he might perfectly well do so.

Dan heard voices and footsteps. He heard doors opening and closing. Quick as a blink he was out of the window and clinging to the drainpipe beside it. He closed the window from outside. He could not close the catch; he did not think anybody would notice. He went up the drain-pipe and over the gutter to the roof. There was no bellow from the policeman below. The roof was tiled and fairly steep. Dan did not attempt to go up it. He lay on his face on the tiles, his feet in the gutter, invisible except from a helicopter.

He heard the bumping of the search below him, the sound muffled by the insulation of the roof. The bumping receded. Covert drawn blank. Whole house drawn blank. What would they think? Obviously, that Dan had got away out of the house just before the police car arrived.

All that the police, these particular police, were on to was one stolen car. It had been appalling folly to leave it outside the nursing home. He should have left it a mile away and done the rest on foot.

What? Arrive on foot, at a house miles from anywhere, when he was pretending to be a rich man? Yes, he should have said his car had broken down. . . . He had been a bit slapdash. It came of being up all night, and then missing his morning nap. He needed a nap now, very badly indeed. It was not a project to contemplate, not on a roof as steep as this.

The sun had gone down behind the woods. There was no more sunshine in the nurse's little room, nor on Dan's roof, although the tops of trees were still brilliant with it. Dan discovered another disadvantage of his position. He had not brought an overcoat. He had not got one that went with his banker's suit. It was already at the edge of freezing. The roof and the drainpipe would be slippery with frost, and his hands too numb to grip. To wait until dark and then climb down would be insanely risky.

The top floor of the house had been searched. It was safe for him, if he was careful and lucky.

Dan slid down into a crouch on the edge of the roof. He peered over the gutter, not altogether trusting the gutter, careful to keep his centre of gravity as far as possible on the roof. He did not much trust the tiles, either. A number were cracked. The policeman was still there. Another cold bloke. But he did have a greatcoat.

It was beginning to get dark, but it was by no means full dark. Dan dared wait no longer. He hoped he was not already too cold to climb. Lying on his stomach, he let himself slide inch by inch down the roof, using the friction of his front on the tiles, using the gutter as much as he dared, until he could grope with his legs for the down-pipe and wrap them round it.

He was not doing his best suit much good.

He transferred his weight to the drainpipe, and slithered a couple of feet down it. There was no light in the nurse's window. He had a titanic struggle, pushing up the lower half of the sash wndow. At least nobody had done up the catch.

Dan climbed into the little room. He shut the window quickly. Though dark, the little room was still warm. The warmth was marvellous after the cruel, beautiful frosty evening. Dan felt overwhelming gratitude, to whatever saint looks after poachers, that he had safely managed the climb and that the window had not been locked. He felt a wave of bottomless fatigue. Too much had happened in the last twenty hours. He was puzzled by the present and frightened by the future. He felt his legs unable to support him. He thought he must sit down for a moment, and then make a plan and get away from this depressing and oddly heartwarming place.

He sat down on the edge of the little high bed. It was bliss to sit. He lay back, sternly telling himself that it could only be for a minute.

His mind bumped round in exhausted circles. Whoever had sent Edgar Bland to Cobb Wood had known about Dan, mentioned him. Whoever had cancelled the appointment at the nursing home had known about all that. With his last waking thought Dan knew who had killed Edgar Bland.

Juanita Jones had only been in love, really in love, twice in her life.

The first boy was black like herself. It was at the college in Bermuda, when she was still living with the English clergyman who had brought her up and given her his name, although the Joneses had never adopted her and she came from quite another country. The Reverend Athelstan Jones had been very shocked, coming home unexpectedly and finding Juanita with her blouse unbuttoned on the settee with her boy. They sent her to England, to the care of Mrs. Jones' sister, and she got a place at Bristol University.

And there she met the second love of her life, a gentle, vague, untidy boy who was supposed to be studying mathematics. Instead he studied Juanita, and also such drugs as were available in the Bristol discos. His university career did not so much terminate as crumble gradually but utterly. Someone who had charge of him sent him off to Australia, to make a man of him. Juanita thought they would make a corpse of him, and her heart was broken. She could no longer bear the university.

The problem was that she was only a legitimate resident of Britain as long as she was enrolled at a recognized place of education. Otherwise she was an illegal immigrant. So she could go home to the Joneses in Bermuda, or to her own country. But she didn't want to. In accent, upbringing and outlook she was an educated Englishwoman.

She solved the problem in the simplest possible way— by hiding. And, in hiding, doing a job that was sometimes heartbreaking but always profoundly worthwhile. Nobody at Rosebank minded what colour she was. They liked her cultivated voice and her warm smile, her deftness and gentleness, her patience in listening.

Juanita had hinted to Matron, because she thought she was morally obliged to do so, that there was a little bit of irregularity in her being in the country at all. Matron had not been the slightest bit concerned. Really good staff were hard to come by. No one was likely to bother them, in such an out-of-the-way place.

The only trouble with her life was loneliness. She had never much liked large parties, but she had liked companionship. She had liked love. The only man at Rosebank under eighty years of age was Stephen. Stephen was kind, but he was not interested in Juanita in that way, and she was not interested in him in that way either. Young men sometimes came to visit their elderly relations, and some of them looked at Juanita in a way she recognized and liked. She sometimes had a chance to talk to a young man visitor, in the hall or in the garden. Nothing ever came of it. Nothing could.

The rest of the staff came and went rather quickly. They were Irish and Pakistani and West Indian. Some of them were very nice women and good nurses, but the place was too quiet for them.

Then Captain Cavendish came. Before his arrival his name had evoked, for Juanita, a tall and swaggering hero in shiny riding boots—something out of the novelettes she had read as a schoolgirl in Bermuda. She was astonished by the gentle little man who stood smiling bashfully at the door. She was astonished by the brilliance of his blue eyes and the extraordinary sweetness of his smile.

He was not much bigger than she was. The thought popped into her head—very shocking, quite out of the blue—that he was just the right height to kiss her. She thought he must have been an odd kind of soldier. The Royal Regiment of Pixies. Princess Juanita's Own Corps of Leprechauns.

Within seconds of their coming face to face—before they had even gone into the house—his smile had broadened from bashfulness into something else. His eyes had flickered up and down her—those amazing eyes of cornflower blue—and his grin was the purest lechery.

When he followed her down the hall, she felt his eyes, like a caress, on her behind.

She might see him again. If he was putting an aunt in Rosebank, she might see him regularly.

Juanita knew that she was being silly as well as shameless, but she let herself enjoy a little daydream. It was because she was bored and lonely. It was because of those eyes and that gentle, lecherous, appreciative smile.

She was a bit of a mess, after the marathon of getting some of the old things to eat up their lunches. Not immediately needed for anything, she ran upstairs to her room to tidy up.

She told herself it was her duty to Rosebank, to Matron, to the patients. She knew it was because she was hoping to see Captain Cavendish.

While she was upstairs, the police arrived. They told the most extraordinary story. He was not Captain, or Cavendish. He had stolen his car. If he was the man the police thought he might be, he was a dangerous and violent criminal on the run. They searched the house. They even looked under the beds of all the old patients. They saw some pretty odd things there. They searched Juanita's room, which took about two seconds. Nobody could understand where he had got to, how he had got away.

Of course it was very wrong to be a dangerous criminal—Juanita had departed from some of the rules of the Reverend Athelstan Jones, but her attitude was basically respectable. But she found she was delighted this particular criminal had got away. She hoped he would go on getting away. In any case it was impossible that he was dangerous. He had the least dangerous eyes she had ever seen. In one way. In another, they were most dangerous eyes she had ever seen.

She was a sort of fugitive herself. One fugitive ought to help another. Given the chance, she would have done so without hesitation. It was lucky, she thought, reproving herself, that this was entirely academic.

It came time to give the patients their suppers and their baths. It was tiring. Many of them were fretful and rebellious, tired at the end of the day though they had done so little. Matron's patience was truly wonderful. Juanita tried conscientiously to follow that splendid example.

She would have liked, that evening, to go out, almost anywhere, with almost anybody. But there was nowhere to go, and no means of transport, and above all no one to go with.

After her own supper, in the little bare, bright staff dining room, she went forlornly up to her room. She would read some more of *Le Rouge et le Noir*, struggling with the French; it was too overpoweringly gloomy to be exactly enjoyable, but at least it was very, very long.

She went into her room and turned on the light. She opened her mouth to scream, but no scream came out. Something utterly impossible had happened. It was the impossibility that shook Juanita, more than the fact, which was simply that the man she had been daydreaming about was lying, fully dressed, fast asleep on her bed.

The light woke him. He opened his eyes. They were even bluer than Juanita remembered.

Juanita shut the door, wondering where her duty lay.

"So sorry to gate-crash," said the man who was not called Captain Cavendish. "I'm afraid I dropped off."

"But they searched!" said Juanita.

"I was on the roof."

"Oh. They ought to have thought of that. Are you really a violent criminal?"

He smiled. His eyes flickered up and down her as he smiled. He sat up, his hair rumpled, his face still softened by sleep.

He said, "You're a nurse, a trained judge of human nature. *Am* I a dangerous violent criminal?"

Juanita meant to frown, but, in response to that lovely, lecherous, sleepy smile, she felt her own huge and immodest grin.

"But," she said, still feeling on her face the grin which did not go with what she was saying, "you are running away from the police."

"Ah, they think I did something I didn't do."

"Idiots."

"Not altogether. They can be forgiven for thinking the way they do. I'd jump to the same conclusion myself. Still, just before I began to enjoy the hospitality of your bed, it came to me what must have actually happened."

"Then," said Juanita, "all you have to do is prove it."

"Yes," said the man who wasn't Captain Cavendish. "Yes . . ."

He scratched his rumpled head. Juanita wanted to stroke it. She almost had to clutch her hands together behind her back, to stop herself reaching one out to him.

She was not a nurse, as he had said, but she thought she was a good judge of human nature. Supremely obviously this gentle, fascinating little man was not a violent criminal.

He said, "Can I get out of the house without being seen?"

"Yes," said Juanita, with a stab of disappointment. "Do you want to go now?"

"I'd like a bath and something to eat," he said, "but I don't suppose I can impose on your hospitality."

"Of course you can," said Juanita. "I can creep down to the kitchen and get you some leftovers. It'll be cold. I don't think I can heat it up."

"You're a grand girl. The moment I saw you, I hoped I'd get a chance to talk to you. I didn't expect to dine with you. Or . . ."

"Or what?" said Juanita.

"Have a tête-à-tête in a bedroom."

Juanita giggled. She was amazed at herself, and at everything that was happening.

As she expected, the kitchen staff were off home or watching the telly in the patients' lounge. She piled a plate with cold cottage pie, sprouts and boiled potatoes, and got upstairs again unseen.

Then she saw a light under Maeve Byrne's door, next door to the bathroom on the top floor.

Dan Mallett (a name that suited him far better than Cavendish) rose politely to his feet when she came into her room. He took the plate from her, grinned, put it on the tiny dressing-table, put his hands on her shoulders, and kissed her on the cheek.

"Oh," she said, feeling another big silly grin on her face.

He said, "I haven't eaten for twelve hours, and until I do I'm good for nothing. I haven't had a proper wash, either, so I should think I'm pretty antisocial in a confined space."

"There's a bathroom down the passage. But there's a

77

problem. Only one other person sleeps on this floor, but her room is next to the bathroom and she's there. She can hear the bath running. And footsteps going up and down the passage. I can't have two baths."

"Ah. You need a bath, Juanita?"

"After giving Mrs. Parker her supper, I certainly do."

"We'll face that problem when I'm feeling stronger. Which will be almost immediately, thanks to you."

He ate delicately, but with a voracious appetite. His manners were as good as Matron's, his intake ten times as much. While he ate he asked Juanita about herself, and she found herself telling him her life story.

"I'm rather a funny mixture, you see," she said. "An English student, a Bermudan orphan, but actually a Nicaraguan, and a fugitive from justice like you."

"Different shape," said Dan, with the grin Juanita was now getting used to. "Will your friend down the passage come out of her room to talk to you?"

"No. She might call out, but she's in bed by now."

"Then we go down the passage together, exactly in step. One lot of footsteps. Very crafty device, not original. Then we run one nice big bath."

"Oh," said Juanita.

"How big is the bath?"

"Oh," said Juanita.

She was proud of her body, but nothing in her life had prepared her for its glory that night.

They had their first passionate kiss when they were both covered in soapsuds, kneeling facing one another in eight inches of steaming water.

They had their fiftieth in her bed, after a miracle of lovemaking which made her smile through her tears, and weep through her laughter.

6

DAN SET his mental alarm clock to wake him half an hour before dawn. It worked, and found him utterly puzzled. He was in a strange bed, and apparently sharing it with a small, warm, naked, sleeping girl.

With memory came a flood of gratitude and affection and respect. Juanita was taking a terrific risk, of the sack, of bad trouble with the police, of expulsion from the country. Probably her parson in Bermuda would not take her back, so she would have to go to some appalling shanty-town in Nicaragua, to people she didn't know, with whom she had nothing in common. She knew all that as well as he did. She had known all along the risk she was taking. She had taken it because she was kind and because she liked him. He liked her, too. He liked her very much indeed.

He woke her up by kissing her nose, and told her so.

She wriggled sleepily in his arms. He could not see her smile in the dark, but he could feel it under his own lips.

Later he found himself with his head pillowed, in blissful comfort, on her firm little breast.

He murmured, "I must go before daylight."

"Yes, I know. I wish you could stay. Anyway you must come back."

"Do you really want me to, Juanita? A violent criminal like me?"

He felt under his cheek the giggle that vibrated her diaphragm.

"For a girl that doesn't want a man to come back," she said, "I'm behaving in a pretty odd way."

"I like the way you behave," said Dan. "I like everything about you."

"Where will you go now? How will you prove somebody else killed that man?"

Dan paused before replying. He trusted both Juanita's loyalty and her good sense. She would give him away neither deliberately nor by mistake. But suppose somebody discovered where he had spent the night. Suppose the police asked her a lot of questions, with the threat always there, spoken or unspoken, of sending her back to her birthplace. She had better not know where he was going, or whom he suspected.

"I'll try to go home," he said. "Where I go then depends on what happens."

"You must stay hidden."

"I'm good at that."

"But you can't lie out under a hedge in this weather."

"There's barns and stables and things."

"There's here. It's nicer than a stable. I'm nicer than a cow."

"What about night duty?"

"Every third night. Not tomorrow, but the next night."

"It's terribly tempting."

"It's obvious, darling. It's the one perfectly safe place for you. Nobody ever comes in here."

"Cleaners?"

"Good gracious no, not up here. I do it. Give way to the temptation, Dan. I never do, as you know, but I think you ought to."

"I'm frightened of what might happen to you."

"I'm not. Nothing can."

He promised to come back, if and when he could. She said she would leave the window unlatched so that he could always climb in. But what he said was true—he was frightened of what might happen to her.

It was also true that he did not want to lose her so soon after finding her. He was enchanted by the combination of the cook, educated personality, and the wriggling, enthusiastic little body.

He did not at all want to leave her warm bed and her warm arms for the freezing dawn, but he forced himself out of bed and into his inadequate clothes. He went out of the window and on to the drainpipe. Clinging to the drainpipe with one hand, he stretched out the other hand to where he thought she was in the pitch-dark open window. He felt his fingers touch her head; he felt her take his hand and kiss it.

Moved, he went down the drainpipe. The metal was so cold under his hands that it felt as though it were burning. He went as quietly as he could. He tried to save his best suit from yet more damage, but he thought he would never again be able to impersonate a bank manager in it.

The grass, starched by the frost, crackled under his feet when he reached the ground. He prowled round to the front of the house. There were a few lights behind curtained windows—the night staff, and unspeakable minor crises to one or two old patients. A light washed dimly out over the gravel where the Mercedes had been. No doubt it was now back at Medwell Court.

There must be at least one car belonging to Rosebank. Stephen was probably chauffeur as well as everything else. But Dan would not take a car from people he so much respected.

He set off for Quimbury, remembering the way without difficulty in the dark, although he had done it only the other way, in a car, by daylight.

He walked all the way into Quimbury, his face and hands and feet getting very cold. The sky was beginning to pale. There were a few cars parked in the streets. They were all locked. Without rancour, Dan cursed the mistrustful people of the village. Picking locks was something he had never learned; it was knowledge he would have liked, but he did not know where to go for instruction.

He found a lady's bicycle in the porch of a modern bungalow. It was padlocked, with a large chain. But the lady had put the chain round the frame of the bicycle, not between the spokes of a wheel. It looked wonderfully secure but it was functionless. Dan blessed impractical ladies who put chains uselessly on their bicycles.

Parts of him got quite hot as he bicycled home to Medwell. But his extremities were very cold.

He crossed the river by the fisherman's footbridge a mile above the village. He still had the world to himself. The river slid like a piece of dull steel under his feet. There was no birdsong. The only sound was the small grasshopper clicking of the bicycle as he wheeled it over

82

the bridge. He went carefully, alert, looking and listening.

He saw no people, but he saw instead something which completely baffled him. On the bank at the very edge of the water, twenty yards upstream of the bridge, some kind of party was going on. A group of small animals seemed to be dancing round something. Dan could not see what animals they were, or what they were dancing round.

He had to get on. But he had to see what was going on.

As the light gradually strengthened, he saw that the object in the middle was a fish. It was a big rainbow trout, a three-pounder. The little animals were not dancing round it but eating it. They were in continual movement, each one dashing in, biting a piece off the fish, dodging back again to chew and swallow.

What were the animals? Not stoats. Not polecats. Not baby otters. Not any animals Dan had ever seen before. It came to him suddenly that they were mink, escaped from a farm and most successfully running wild, several thousand miles from home. He watched, fascinated, knowing that he ought to get on, reluctant to miss this show nature was putting on for him.

There were four small mink and one much bigger one. Obviously a parent and a litter. (Was litter right for mink?) The small ones were not babies but adolescents, extremely strong and active for their size. As Dan watched, the full-grown one seemed to withdraw a little from the feast. It seemed to Dan that she was moving tactfully, anxious not to spoil the party. He knew it was ridiculous and sentimental to ascribe such motives to an animal—especially a vicious little predator like a mink—

83

but still he was sure the adult was taking care to move away without the others noticing.

He realised why. The mink was some sort of cousin of the weasel, and it was doing what a parent weasel did at this time of year—having taught its young how to kill and to survive, it crept away, when they were having breakfast, and left them to fend for themselves.

Dan was so interested that he did not notice, for a moment, how cold he was getting from standing still. He moved. The young mink all instantly disappeared. He wondered if they would find their mother again, or if she had successfully eluded them, but he was too cold to worry much about it.

He went on over the footbridge, remounted the bicycle, and headed for the Priory Woods. His hands were almost too cold to hold the handlebars.

Mink probably killed and ate their old, he thought. There were no Rosebanks or Matrons in mink society. He did not think there were many in human society, either. Matron would never be able to afford a mink coat. Dan vaguely wondered what her real name was. Perhaps the individual was lost in the function—she was simply Matron.

A police car was parked outside his cottage. Of course it was. They were waiting for Edgar Bland's murderer. Nothing could have been predicted with more certainty.

He wanted to change into warmer and rougher clothes. It might be possible, if a policeman was snoring in a chair in the front room. But there might be a policeman in Dan's bed. Probably they wouldn't be as sensible as that, but it was what Dan himself would have done. A change of clothes was not worth the risk of climbing through the window into the arms of the law.

Crossly, Dan decided to lie up during the day, and get into Medwell Court in the evening. Major March was there. Mrs. March was not there. This was Peggy's information and it was undoubtedly correct. Peggy herself was there part-time. Dan didn't think she'd scream for the police if she saw him. That might depend on what she'd been hearing. It was a risk he had to take, because he had to know about telephone calls.

There were plenty of places where he could lie up safe and warm and well fed, looked after by girls who trusted him no matter what anyone said, or girls who didn't trust him an inch, but still couldn't resist whatever it was about him that they liked. (It was a perpetual mystery to Dan why a little runt with a bad reputation should be so lucky with girls.) The difficulty was getting to any of the places without being seen by eyes less tolerant. The husbands or fathers or employers of the girls all knew Dan by sight and by reputation. Some of them had threatened him with a charge of buckshot in the backside if he ever came near their houses. And all of them knew by now, a village being a village, that the police were after him for killing Edgar Bland with a crossbow.

He might have been better in Juanita's bed all day. But he had wanted a change of clothes.

The sun was high now, and there was just enough warmth in it to melt the frost where it struck. There was not enough to do Dan any good. He shivered as he wondered where to go. He wanted his breakfast and his morning nap.

In the end he settled for Willie Martin's hay barn. It was the least uncomfortable place he could get to safely: or, putting it another way, the least unsafe place that was moderately comfortable. The leafless hedgerows gave him cover enough, and the bicycle was safely hidden until he wanted it again. He thought he must be a ridiculous sight, crawling about the country in a torn and grubby banker's suit, his little black shoes scuffed with frozen mud.

Willie Martin was taking hay from the south end of his open-sided Dutch barn to feed his cows. Dan would be undisturbed on top of the bales in the north end. He climbed up and made a nest for himself, cutting the binder twine of a couple of bales so that he could lie soft. The unbaled hay would taste just as good to the cows. He was not robbing Willie Martin of anything, although he would have been quite agreeable to doing so.

With a mattress and an eiderdown of soft hay, Dan was soon warm and snug. The stuff was a wonderful insulator. When Dan's mother cooked porridge in the old-fashioned way, keeping it warm all night, she put the pot in a nest of hay in a tea chest. Dan felt like a pot of porridge, a pot in a banker's suit.

He went to sleep wondering how he could prove what he knew to be the truth about the murder, and wishing that Juanita was snuggled up in the hay beside him.

He woke up in the middle of the afternoon, wanting his lunch and his tea as well as his breakfast. There was a certain muffled commotion at the far end of the barn: voices, and the thudding of a tractor. Willie Martin was loading hay onto a trailer. There was no reason they should bother Dan, or he them, unless they set fire to the barn. He lay as snug as a fieldmouse in the warmth of his cocoon of hay, feeling, for the thousandth time, a little glow of joy that the job of heaving hay bales was taken on by somebody else.

86

The glow of joy disappeared when he remembered why he was there.

The timbre of the tractor's engine changed as it was put into gear. It bumped away over the frost-bound bumps in the cart track. Dan lay still for a little longer, as unwilling as in the dawn to exchange warmth and comfort and safety for whatever now faced him.

He emerged from his nest at last, and satisfied himself that he was alone with the hay bales. He climbed down, and tried to brush the hay off his suit and out of his hair. Covered in wisps of hay, his banker's suit was more incongruous than ever. He glumly faced the necessity of buying a new one. He faced the chance, which seemed a pretty good chance, of never needing a new one.

Keeping well clear of Willie Martin and his boys, he made his inconspicuous way to Medwell Court.

He tried to plan as he went. He must catch Peggy Bowman alone. That was the first and most obvious necessity. He must ask her about telephone calls made forty-eight hours before, and about one other crucial matter. He must have this conversation in a place from which he could run away very quickly, and hide very completely, just in case somebody else saw him, or Peggy herself began screaming and blowing whistles.

The pigeon-loft was the place.

But it was not the place. To Dan's surprise the birds had all been fed, much earlier than usual: the Turbits, affectionate and cheeky birds with the most attractive personalities of all fancy pigeons, white with striking coloured wings, and the Oriental Frills, of which Major March had the type called Blondinettes, red-laced and sulphur-laced, smaller headed than the Turbits but with similar ridiculous beaks. Dan wondered how they managed to eat corn with them. What they couldn't do was feed their squabs with them, so the loft also housed Rollers and West of England Tumblers whose only function was to act as foster parents to the exotics.

Dan looked at them all appreciatively, as he so often had. He respected the way they ate exactly as much as they needed, then waddled across the floor of the loft to their water pots and had a little drink to wash the grain down, never thereafter going back for more food. They looked silly, but they were a lot more sensible than people. Dan knew this was not an original reflection, but it was one that came to him constantly.

Dan supposed Peggy had fed the birds early in order to get away early. It was a blow. He scratched his head in perplexity, wondering whether to try to see her in her own house, or do some fossicking round in Medwell Court, or go straight back to Rosebank and Juanita, or try again to get into his own cottage. . . .

Dan saw Peggy's moped. It was in the most absurd place, perched on its stand between a big antique wrought-iron garden seat and a topiary yew. He could see it from the loft, looking almost straight down, but it would be invisible from the house or from anywhere in the garden. . . . Of course. It was hidden. Peggy usually propped it by the side door which was handy for Major March's office. Anyone seeing that the moped was not there would know she had gone away home. She had not gone away home, but she wanted everyone to think so. She wanted Major March to think so. Why? Was she joining Dan's profession? And she an ex-solicitor's secretary? Nipping off with a collection of snuffboxes or medals or money from the safe? If so, the place she had picked to hide her moped was a very silly one. Other people might not come into the pigeon loft, but Major March did. He loved his birds. Nothing was more likely than an evening inspection. He was just as likely to glance down, casually, as Dan was. And there was the unmistakable moped, bright yellow, with a white plastic carrier on the back, and Peggy's L-plates back and front.

The moped was there quite innocently, because somebody had said it looked vulgar to have a yellow moped by the side door of a grand country house. That fitted with Major March.

No, it didn't. He was a coarse-grained, ostentatious, phoney kind of man, but he wasn't a stupid old woman. He wouldn't order Peggy to hide her moped under a yew. Dan's first guess must be right. Peggy was in the house. Presumably, therefore, Major March was not in the house. She was taking advantage of her knowledge of his movements. Right, if she was alone in the house except for servants far away, Dan could have his little talk with her. And if he caught her doing something peculiar, she couldn't blab about him in case he blabbed about her.

Dan's position was better than he thought, better than he had dared to hope.

He came down out of the loft, and crept like a spider to the house. It was still daylight but getting darker. It was getting colder by the second. There were lights in the back part of the house. Somebody was washing up tea, or beginning to cook dinner. The thought made Dan feel quite ill with hunger. Juanita's cold cottage pie was an awful long time ago.

Alert for gardeners or anybody else, Dan crept round the side of the house, keeping close to the wall. He could

89

not be seen from a window unless somebody leaned right out. It was not an evening for leaning out of windows. He went to the side door, where Peggy's moped was usually to be seen. He did not know where Major March's office was—only that it was near this door. A window near the door was heavily curtained, although there was still brightness in the sky. Dan tried to peep through a crack in the curtains. There was no crack. He thought he heard voices, but it was difficult to be sure.

He did not think the door would be locked so early in the evening, though no doubt it was locked at night. He did not want to go through the door into a house utterly strange to him, but where everybody knew his face, and knew that he was wanted for murder.

He turned the handle of the door, very slowly. He pushed fractionally. It was not locked. He was almost disappointed. He had almost wanted to be locked out. He opened the door a crack, enough to see if there was light inside. It was dark inside. He went in, shutting the door behind him. He was in a stone-flagged passage. From round the corner at the end of the passage came some light, and from under the door to his right came a small crack of light. That was the room with the curtained window. Maybe Peggy was alone in there, helping herself from the safe. If so, it was the right place for Dan, and the sooner the better. But it was easy to resist the impulse to open the door and march in.

Dan tried to look through the keyhole and he tried to listen. He could see nothing. The keyhole was covered on the inside, or there was a key in it. He heard movements. There was someone in the room. Something fell. It might have been a book. It sounded like the weight of a book, landing with a thud on a carpet. Peggy was a careless burglar. There was another thud. Another book?

Dan crept down the passage, soundless on the flag-stones, to the next door. There was no light below it, no sound beyond it. Through the keyhole Dan saw the bright oblong of an uncurtained window. He opened the door and slipped into the room. It was a sort of flower room or utility room, with gumboots and sticks and a few expensive, amateurish garden tools. It connected with the first room, which Dan took to be the office.

The connecting door had a more accommodating key-hole. It was a big, old-fashioned keyhole. What Dan saw was a complete surprise to him, but after half a second he realised that it should have been no surprise at all. It was the supremely obvious explanation of everything that had been puzzling him. Everything fell into place. It confirmed the rightness of his guess, and filled in all the reasons.

Major March, in his shirt-sleeves, was sitting in an armchair beside his desk. His shirtfront was unbuttoned. His big, purplish face was for the moment invisible, but the greying black hairs on his chest were obtrusively visible.

On his lap was Peggy Bowman. Her boots were on the floor. They were the bumps. Her sweater was round her neck and her bra was undone. Major March's face was hidden between her big pink breasts.

Major March began to pull the sweater over Peggy's head, so that her face too disappeared. When it re-appeared it looked pretty cheerful. She began to undo some more of Major March's buttons.

They'd be busy for some time yet. They'd only just

started. They must be sure of privacy. If so, Dan was sure of privacy. He could stay where he was for a bit, though he did not want to watch any more.

This was why the pigeons had been fed early.

This was why Peggy's moped was hidden between the garden seat and the yew.

Peggy was bored with old George Bowman, and as Dan himself had cause to know she was attracted by money and success. Major March had plenty of both.

Mrs. March was a shrill, shrivelled creature. Peggy's bouncing pink breasts would make a nice change for the Major. No doubt he was pretty generous. There was nothing in the least unusual or surprising about any of it. It had probably been going on for some time—probably from the moment Peggy had started working at the Court. She was not one to be coy.

Major March was terribly sensitive about his reputation. He was said to have ideas about going into politics. That was one of the reasons he worked so hard at being popular.

What had happened was that Edgar Bland had found out. He was a sneaking, spying sort of man in a pheasant covert and outside it. Maybe he had peeped through this very keyhole, or caught them at it out of doors somewhere. (Dan remembered that Peggy, unlike many girls afraid of snakes or spiders, liked it out of doors if the sun was hot.)

Edgar Bland had blackmailed Major March. Probably not for huge sums, but enough to pay for those hideous new trappings Dan had seen in his cottage. Beryl had said Major March had given Edgar Bland a generous bonus. So he had. That was how it would appear in the bank statement, too. And if Major March was asked about those payments to Edgar Bland, he'd simply say—I gave him a bonus. Edgar Bland was a good gamekeeper. A man's allowed to give a good bonus to his gamekeeper.

And then Edgar Bland asked a bit too much. He was approaching retirement. Beryl didn't think he was saving much. He wanted a nice nest egg. This was guesswork but it was terribly convincing.

Then what? Major March knew all about Edgar Bland's appointment at the nursing home. Of course he knew—he gave him permission to go. So he rang up Edgar at home, and pretended to be the nursing home, and cancelled the appointment. Maybe he disguised his voice. Maybe he got somebody else to make the call, an accomplice or somebody who didn't know what he was doing. Maybe Peggy. Dan hoped not. He hoped Peggy knew nothing about it. Of course the call would be untraceable, a short local call going through an automatic exchange.

Then he rang up Edgar Bland again, and told him to go to Cobb Wood. And gave Dan as the reason. He knew that would get Edgar Bland to Cobb Wood in the middle of the night as surely as a sackful of gold. Well, almost as surely.

Maybe he already owned a crossbow. Maybe he bought one in a big, busy London shop, where nobody would know him or remember him.

And in the morning he rang up the Milchester police. An anonymous call. Voice disguised, or the accomplice again. Body by Cobb Wood, Dan Mallett seen on the spot. Poacher defending himself against a gamekeeper with a grudge. That must have happened for the police car to get there so quickly.

Trying to test this theory for holes, Dan heard bumps and giggles from the next room. In no spirit of prurience, but simply to see how much time he had, he glanced through the keyhole again. They had taken off the rest of their clothes. They were on the floor. It was a nice thick carpet. Peggy was underneath. Dan thought this unchivalrous of the Major. He looked away quickly. The Major's upreared buttocks were a horrible yellowish colour.

Dan could find no holes in his theory. Motive and method—it all fitted like a jigsaw.

But what could anybody prove? What could the whole of Scotland Yard prove? Dan could testify that the Major was having an affair with Peggy Bowman. That would do the Major very little harm, except for annoying his wife and Peggy's husband, and maybe putting a bit of a check on his political ambitions. Beryl could testify that Edgar Bland had been getting some extra money. Right, nice generous bonus for a faithful servant nearing retirement.

What you had to prove was that the Major made those three telephone calls, two to Edgar and one to the police. If nobody heard him, and he dialled the number, how in God's name could you prove that?

Dan had read about perfect crimes. He reckoned Major March had committed one. He did not altogether blame him for killing Edgar Bland. It was not a thing Dan himself would have done, but blackmail was a dirty trick. What was unforgivable was putting the blame on Dan. That was a dirty trick too.

And now Major March, with blood on his hands, was enjoying his piece of pastry without guilt or remorse, and without Edgar Bland. While Dan was crawling all over the countryside, with the whole population looking for him. It was an unfair situation. It should be reversed.

Dan had not the slightest idea what to do.

7

REASSURED, though distracted, by the continuing grunt-ings on the other side of the door, Dan thought harder than he had ever thought before.

It might be possible to prove that Major March made telephone calls at the relevant times. Peggy or a servant might have seen him doing so, or heard the ping at the end of the call, if he rang from here; someone else might have seen him if he called from somewhere else.

So what? There were a million legitimate reasons for a rich, busy, hospitable man to use the telephone. Even if Dan could prove that the Major had been making calls at the precise moment that the two calls came to Edgar Bland and the one in the morning to the police—and that was a million to one against—it proved only that the Ma-jor used what he was paying for. He might have made other calls at the same times, which would be remem-bered, by which he could explain his use of the tele-phone. If he was a careful man he would do that. Dan thought the Major would be a very careful man when he was murdering somebody.

Dan despaired of catching the Major by way of the telephone calls, if he had made them himself. How about an accomplice? Peggy? Peggy was threatened by Edgar Bland, too, if she cared about her marriage to George. But Dan was certain that Peggy was too essentially friendly, too law-abiding and respectable (however often she opened her legs) to be a deliberate accomplice in a murder, even of a blackmailer, and too intelligent to be an unwitting accomplice. The Spanish butler? No, Major March would never take such a risk, never put himself so much into another man's power.

There was no lever to be found in Peggy or the servants or anyone else inside or outside Medwell Court. The lever had to be in Major March himself.

If you went after an animal you studied that animal, tried to think like it, anticipated its reactions and its movements. You studied it, and got inside its head. Dan had studied all kinds of animals, but he had not had much chance to study Major March.

What really did he know about the man? Only what everybody knew, together with what he had just learned. The bonhomie, the lavishness, the big cars and friends with big cars, the tweeds worn like fancy dress, the re-deeming passion for fancy pigeons. Origins? Dan had no idea. The Major was fairly obviously not sprung from a long line of old Etonian landowners. He was some sort of financier or entrepreneur. He was not a major in the sense that Admiral Jenkyn was an admiral: he had prob-ably been in the Pay Corps in the second half of the war. No doubt the rank had helped him in business, as it helped him with the nobs and near-nobs of the country-side. It was all a bit fragile, Dan thought—the rank in the army and the rank on the social ladder. It made him more vulnerable to an Edgar Bland, more desperate to keep what he'd got.

Did the lever lie there? Maybe, but the man was as clever as a fox—he must be, to have made so much money—and the fox was much the cleverest of all the animals Dan knew.

But foxes could be caught. A vixen could be caught with her cubs, simply with a spade. A dog-fox could be caught because it slipped into a routine, like a commuter catching his morning train. . . . If a fox knew there were hens in a coop, he would visit that coop, just casually, just in passing, almost nightly, just in case the farmer's wife had left the door open. She goes off somewhere in a hurry, the car breaks down—and in the morning the coop's full of corpses. Was that any help? Was there a pattern in Major March's behaviour which could be used to catch him?

Not in detail. In general, yes—he murdered black-mailers. But he wouldn't do it a second time with a cross-bow by Cobb Wood.

But he did murder blackmailers. Dan was in a position to blackmail him. Dan could threaten to tell Mrs. March, and George Bowman, and the County Conservative Asso-ciation, what he had seen through the keyhole. He could ask a lot of money, really a lot, not once but again and again. Major March wouldn't go to the police. If that was how he reacted, he would have reacted that way before. But he hadn't shopped Edgar Bland. He'd shot him. He'd shoot Dan, too, or pulp his skull with a crowbar or drown him or burn him alive. A predictable reaction. That was certain enough to use as the basis of a plan.

Dan drafted in his mind the letter he would write to Major March. He found it a little sickening.

The Major must be made to try to kill Dan. But it was quite important to Dan that he should not succeed. It was also important that a witness saw the whole thing. Place and time must therefore be of Dan's choosing, with the witness in position in advance and well hidden.

There was a good deal to be thought out, and the sooner the better.

A long, shuddering sigh came through the connecting door. Then a cough, Peggy's cough. Dan recognized it. It was a little, prim cough, saying that they'd finished and life had returned to normal.

Dan glanced through the keyhole. Peggy was sitting up, pulling on her tights. The Major was dressing, too, standing bashfully with his back to her. All passion was spent. Dan wondered if he paid her there and then, and if so how much; but he did not wait to see. He slipped out of the room and out of the house.

He waited for Peggy, crouched by the moped below the pigeon loft. It was full dark and very cold. Dan waited for a long time by the moped, wishing he had borrowed a coat from Major March.

A light came and went, just out of his sight, as the side door was opened and closed.

Dan would have to grab Peggy from behind, and put his hand over her mouth. Otherwise she would certainly scream, being accosted by someone popping up out of the darkness.

He heard a car start, and saw the swing of headlights. Major March was giving Peggy a lift home. Fair enough, after he'd kept her working late. George Bowman wouldn't wonder about it.

Dan prowled away round the back of the stables and into the park. He walked among sleepy cattle. He had not managed to talk to Peggy, but he thought that, on balance, he had had a thoroughly successful evening. He knew all the important facts. He had a strategy. It was a question now simply of staying out of sight, staying alive, and getting Major March to try to kill him in front of a witness.

Juanita Jones had to fight, all day, against the silly smile that kept invading her face. She was a conscientious girl, and genuinely concerned about the old people at Rosebank, but it was impossible to keep her mind on her job. She made beds wrong, she swept the same piece of floor half a dozen times, she gave Mrs. Metcalfe two pieces of cake at teatime, so that Miss Nickson got no piece of cake, and a terrible bust-up threatened. It was lucky that, at the time, old Mr. Fortescue had visitors, and Matron and Stephen were both in Mr. Fortescue's room with them, and Juanita hushed up the quarrel before anybody noticed.

Juanita was glad for Mr. Fortescue's sake, as well as for her own, that people had come to see him. They were the first visitors he had had in his four months at Rosebank. If he had any family they were far away, or else they simply didn't care. He was very lonely and very bored. He was virtually bedridden, but his mind was quite sharp. He was well able, Juanita understood, to look after his own affairs. His affairs consisted simply of paying his fees at Rosebank. Unlike almost all the other patients, he was still allowed his chequebook. He was partly blind but he could write a cheque. He always questioned every item on the monthly bill. There were very few items, but he grumbled at the cost of the laundry.

Juanita glimpsed his visitors when they arrived at about three. They were middle-aged men in dark suits. They had briefcases. They were seeing Mr. Fortescue on business. Matron and Stephen joined them, probably to explain about Mr. Fortescue's health or about the costs of Rosebank. Matron would get into a terrible muddle explaining about oil and wages, but Stephen would be good at explaining.

After his visitors had gone, Matron spent quite a long time with Mr. Fortescue. That was so that he should not feel too forlorn at being deserted. A part of Juanita's mind took in all this, but another part could not stop thinking of Dan. She was amazed at him and at herself. Nothing in Bermuda, nothing at Bristol University, nothing at Rosebank had prepared her for anything like Dan. She had not known such a man existed, so gentle, clever, amusing, secret, independent; she did not think any other such man did exist. He was unique, his eyes and his hair and his wedge-shaped face and his small, wiry body that had such an electric effect on her own body.

As to her own behaviour, she was a bit aghast. She could not believe she could give herself to a total stranger, within minutes of finding him in her bedroom. She was simply not that kind of girl. She had more pride, more discrimination.

She couldn't have done it. It was awful that she'd done it. She couldn't wait to do it again. She passionately hoped Dan would come back that night and every other night.

In the evening Juanita heard Mr. Fortescue calling "Veronica!", calling for Matron, as most of the old gentlemen did. It was terribly impressive how much she meant to them, how much comfort and companionship she gave them.

Juanita felt like calling out for Dan. She wanted his comfort and companionship.

Dan was tempted to take Major March's Mercedes

again. It would have been a distinctly saucy gesture. Too saucy. Too risky altogether.

He still wanted a word with Peggy Bowman, but that was too risky too.

He went back to the Priory Woods, and confirmed his gloomy surmise that the police would still be camped in his cottage. He got his borrowed lady's bicycle out of its hiding place, and headed for Quimbury.

He hid the bicycle in the woods which bordered Rosebank's straggling garden. He had no difficulty with Juanita's drainpipe, and she herself was there to open her window. She seemed very pleased to see him. The excited white grin in the little black face seemed to light up the room like a lighthouse.

She fed him again, on perfectly adequate leftovers from the staff supper, and they shared a nice hot bath. Juanita sang in the bath. She sang bits of opera, in a small, husky contralto. Dan had difficulty keeping quiet. But a duet in the bathroom would have surprised the nurse in the next-door bedroom.

Later they lay side by side, snug and happy and relaxed, and Juanita sleepily wondered aloud what had happened to her morals.

Dan tried to pay attention to everything she said, because he thought that of all the many things he owed her, politeness was not the least. But his problems distracted him. He needed an occasion and a location for Major March's attempt to murder him which fulfilled two crucial conditions. One was that he failed; the other was that someone saw him try.

Also there was no time to waste. Dan reckoned he could survive indefinitely with Juanita's food and her

101

bathroom and her bed, and she thought so too. But his mother could not survive indefinitely.

Maybe she'd got the police sawing up firewood and stoking the range. Maybe they were even feeding her. But the food wouldn't be as delicate as what Dan provided.

Every day she tried to manage on her own increased the chance of Dr. Smith taking her away and putting her in a home.

Juanita went to sleep in Dan's arms, as warm and trusting as a puppy. She woke and yawned and giggled.

"Now I'm wide awake," she said. "You get good at catnapping in this job."

"You get good at lots of things," said Dan tightening his arms round her.

Afterwards she was in a mood to talk.

"I don't want to be a bore, or keep you awake," she said, "but I've hardly talked to anybody for months. I mean properly talked like this."

She cross-examined Dan about himself, and he told her as much as she might have found out from anybody in Medwell. She did not call him a liar, but it was clear that she found it extremely difficult to believe a word he said. In her world—the clerical household in Bermuda, the upper-middle-class establishment near Bristol, the university itself—you did not leave a bank once you were in it. Above all you did not put on a broad, comic, rural accent and sweep the ash leaves off people's lawns.

"I thought you weren't like anybody else," she said. "Now I know it. You're not a man at all. You're a different sort of animal. A fox. A little clever fox. A fox cub."

102

"Cubbing," said Dan suddenly.

"What?"

"Sorry to interrupt your analysis of my character. But you've given me an idea. Solved a problem that's been bothering me."

"I'm glad I've been helpful."

Thinking aloud, Dan said, "He's not a hunting man. I don't suppose he even rides. He'll come out if I tell him, but he'll come out on foot. No, wait. He might have had himself taught to ride. That sort often do. He might come out on a hireling. That wouldn't spoil things, but it might make them different. Opening meet in about a fortnight. Much bigger crowd. Too big. Besides, I can't wait that long. I'll find out from the kennels where they're meeting and when. Yes, this is a really good idea. Thank you, love. I do believe you've given me a really good idea."

"I haven't any idea at all," said Juanita. "I mean, of what you're talking about."

"Cat and mouse with the roles reversed," said Dan. "I'm the mouse."

"If there's one thing I hate," she said, "it's people who talk in riddles."

"They'll post people all round the covert," Dan went on thoughtfully, "to head the cubs back in. If you're on foot, you can easily get out of sight of anybody. He'd think he was safe. What he couldn't know was that somebody was watching."

"Who? Watching what?"

"I don't know who. That's another problem. Somebody I can trust."

"It seems to me I'm the only person you can trust."

"I should think that's just about true. But you can't come cub hunting in the middle of the morning on a weekday."

"I probably can. I've never taken any time off. I've never had anything to do."

"And hide in a wood with a murderer prowling about?"

"I'd be very good at that. In a dark wood I'd be invisible. Natural camouflage. I'm a very useful friend for you to have."

"You'd only have to smile and you'd set the wood on fire."

He felt her smile, in the dark, on his bare shoulder. He was surprised that the room was not full of brilliant light from her smile.

She went back to sleep. Dan lay wakeful, considering his idea. To take Juanita as his witness was obviously impossible for a hundred reasons. She might not be believed. The ambiguity of her position would be discovered, with ghastly consequences for herself. And it was too dangerous. It was as bad for Dan to have a dead witness as it was to be dead himself.

Major March would not bring a crossbow out cub hunting, nor any kind of gun. It would be a club or a knife. He might have been trained to use a knife in the army. But to stab someone in the guts or split their skull you had to be close to them. That was why the cub hunting was a good idea—it debarred Major March from methods you could use at a distance.

The whole project was intensely frightening, but Dan could think of no other way to go about it.

The hour before dawn was lovely. Dan felt beautifully refreshed after his sleep and after Juanita. There was no way she could get him anything to eat, but all that she could give him she gave him.

She even had a spare toothbrush.

Dan telephoned the kennels of the Branksford Vale Hunt, from the box outside the post office in Quimbury. He got one or two odd looks from the village people. He used his squire voice to the kennel huntsman. He knew it was not really quite a squire voice; but it was as near to the real thing as Major March's, and near enough for the kennel-huntsman.

He found that hounds were meeting on Monday, Thursday and Saturday, respectively at Ighampton Church, Zeldon Common, and Medwell Priory. At the beginning of the cub hunting season, as soon as most of the harvest was in, in late August, they had met very early in the morning, when there was dew on the ground and the possibility of scent; they packed up in mid-morning, when the sun had dried the ground and the scent, and there was no way either to catch foxes or teach the young hounds how to hunt. On these frosty October mornings there was no need to start so early. Hounds would meet at ten, and probably hunt well into the afternoon.

Dan pondered the three meets, and the working out of his plan.

From Ighampton Church they would draw Hinkney's Wood, a big covert, very suitable for cubbing, an almost certain find. It would suit Dan pretty well, but it was too soon. Major March must be given time for his arrangements, and Dan needed time for letter writing and the recruitment of his witness.

The Thursday meet at Zeldon Common was probably

105

still too soon, and the first draws there were big fields of kale. The enclosures would be entirely surrounded by the mounted field and the foot followers, so that the cubs would be turned back into the kale for the hounds to hunt. A little runt like himself, Dan reflected, could hide in kale as snug as a creepie-crawlie, but it was not a place where Major March would try to kill him, and the middle of a big field was not a place he himself could get away from unseen.

In the effort of catching Major March out, it was not unimportant to remember that he was on the run from the whole countryside for killing Edgar Bland. The whole countryside except Juanita and, to a qualified extent, his mother.

It was Medwell Priory then, the Saturday meet, on his own doorstep. They'd be in the Priory Woods all morning, as long as the scent lasted. Major March must be got there. He must catch sight of Dan when he was out of sight himself. Except for a witness who must be sticking to Dan like corn plaster. Invisible corn plaster.

Dan bought the cheapest available kind of writing paper in the smallest available quantity. He borrowed a ball-point in the post office. He was a little uneasy, parading himself in full view of half Quimbury. He did not think he saw anyone who had any reason to know him. He did not look or talk or act, to anyone who didn't know him well, like a murderous poacher on the run. That was his most important disguise, an air of almost swaggering confidence. It took a bit of keeping up. The bank-manager voice continued excellent camouflage. And Juanita had done her best with his suit, with needle and sponge and brush, and he had rubbed up his little black shoes to something approaching nattiness.

106

Dan wrote in capital letters, with his left hand:

MAJ MARCH

I KNOWS WHAT YOU BEN UP TO WITH PEGY BOWMAN
I SEEN YOU AND SHE AND CAN PROVE SOME TO YOR
WIFE FRENS POLITICKAL BLOKES PEGYS MAN GEORGE
ETC

IM A POOR MAN £1000 USED NOTES FIVES AND TENS
YOUL HARDLY NOTIS

BRING MONY IN SUPERMARKET BAG TO MEDWELL
PRIORY MEET SAT MORNEN LEAV IT IN MIDDLE OF
WOOD WERE I CAN SEE HER

IF YOU ARE NOT THERE OR MONY ARE NOT THER YOR
FUN AND GAMES WILL BE PUBLICK NOWLIGE

IF I PICK HER UP AND SHES CORREC YOUR SECRET IS
SAFE IM NOT GREEDY LIKE POR EDGAR BLAND

A NEEDY FREND

That last gratuitous sentence was crucially important. It
contained a threat. It suggested that the writer knew what
had happened in Cobb Wood and why. It provided
another powerful reason for Major March to kill the writer
of the letter. Equally important, it came near to declar-
ing that the writer was Dan. Major March knew better
than anybody that Dan, and only Dan, had been witness
of Edgar Bland's death. He knew Dan had seen Edgar's
opulent new purchases. Major March was clever enough
to give other people credit for cleverness, and he could do
sums in his head. He would not be quite certain Dan was
the blackmailer, but he would think it highly probable.
He would become certain when he saw Dan in the Priory
Woods on Saturday morning.

At the same time, he would not realize that Dan had

deliberately given himself away as the blackmailer. No blackmailer did that, in the ordinary way. Even Major March was not clever enough to see what Dan was really up to. At least, Dan hoped he wasn't.

Right: He'd try to kill Dan the moment he was sure Dan was the blackmailer. That was quite certain. It was how he reacted to this particular situation. He would conform to his own pattern. Other people in the same circumstance might go to the police, or pay up and keep quiet; he might do either of those things in different circumstances. But in these particular circumstances this particular man would arrive at the meet with a cosh or a commando dagger in his pocket.

He might conceivably bring one thousand pounds in used notes in a plastic supermarket bag. He'd reckon in that event to pay and kill afterwards, as with Edgar Bland. More likely he'd fold up a couple of newspapers. But was it possible that Dan might get his hands on the money, as well as achieving his primary objective?

(Dan caught himself using these fine big words in his mind, as he stood by the postbox with the letter in his hand. He thought his brain was influenced by his suit, and by the voice he had been using in the post office.)

It was a nice dream, £1,000 in cash as well as clearing himself. He allowed himself to dream, as he dropped the letter into the box.

He did not think Major March would make anything of a Quimbury postmark.

108

8

DAN BICYCLED home, on his borrowed lady's bicycle,
furtive as a field mouse, in and out of ditches, as careful as
he could be of his suit, but more careful not to be seen.

As he went, he used the instinctive part of his mind for
steering and for staying out of trouble. He tried to use the
intellectual part for solving the current outstanding problem: who should his witness be, for observing Major
March's attempt to murder him, and for reporting the
attempt accurately and credibly to the police?

There were drawbacks to being a loner.

Most of the people Dan knew well he didn't trust, like
Curly Godden the delinquent cowman. Most of the people he actually trusted didn't trust him, like Dr. Smith in
the village. There were a few people he knew pretty well
and trusted pretty well, like Harry Barnett the water
keeper: but the police wouldn't believe a word Harry
said, not on this sort of thing. Not if it was choosing between Harry's word and Major March's. Harry and Dan
had been at the village school together, before Dan went
on to the Grammar. They'd been wild lads together,
scrumping apples and bird's-nesting and trying to tickle
trout. They were still cronies, as far as a man like Dan had

anything so cosy as a crony. Of course the police would believe that Harry would lie to save Dan. They'd be right. Harry *would* lie to save Dan.

Dan needed somebody as believable as Major March— someone, in the eyes of the police, of the Major's weight and standing. Admiral Jenkyn, the Vicar, Sir George Simpson. Dan pictured himself asking Sir George to hide in the Priory Woods at ten on Saturday morning, to watch Major March attempting murder. The picture was so ludicrous that he almost fell off his bicycle.

He considered the problem, when hiding in ditches permitted, all the way home to his cottage.

He approached the cottage as craftily as always and saw that the bluebottles still swarmed there. It was inevitable. They knew—the Chief Detective Superintendent like a fox knew, and the Detective Sergeant like a Hereford bullock knew—that Dan was concerned about his mother, that he wouldn't leave her for long to fend for herself and the dogs and the birds. They might applaud his concern. But they were bound to make use of it if they could. They thought Dan was a murderer.

Dan abstracted some more cash from the rabbit hole which was his Current Account. He indulged again, briefly, the dream of acquiring on Saturday morning one thousand pounds to add to the Deposit Account in the other and deeper-hidden rabbit hole.

He fished the bicycle out of a thicket, and went by an idiosyncratic route to Ighampton, a sprawling place full of newcomers, a waste of pinkish council houses. In the ordinary way nothing took Dan there. In the ordinary way nothing would drag him there. Consequently nobody

110

knew him there. So it was the place he chose for his shopping.

(Quimbury was all right, too, but Quimbury had been seeing rather a lot of him. If he kept appearing in that village, exotic in his bank-manager's suit and with his clipped bank-manager's voice, people would begin to wonder who he was and where he lived. In a place like that nobody kept speculation to himself. He'd be a talking point in no time, and people would begin to follow his movements.)

He bought what they called "convenience foods" in an Ighampton supermarket. Nobody gave him a second glance. Other browbeaten men were shopping too, for TV snacks and things in batter and things in "gourmet" sauces. Dan tried to look like a husband planning to spend an evening in front of a television set, with a wife who made him do the shopping on his way home from the office. He picked about. Something might tickle his mother's fancy. At least this stuff would be easy for her to get ready, though he guessed some of it might taste pretty odd. He hoped she'd bother. She didn't need much but she needed something.

It occurred to him to buy something for Juanita. But he didn't know what she could do with it. She said Rosebank gave her more than enough to eat. There were always leftovers, or had been until Dan took up residence.

He did buy a flat half-bottle of whisky, which he could carry in his hip pocket.

He went back to his cottage after dark, moving like a grass snake. He piled his purchases where even a policeman would be bound to see them in the morning. They'd

111

know he'd been there. They wouldn't be quite sure. It might be any other well-wisher. But why wouldn't anyone else knock on the door and hand the stuff over? They'd just about know he'd been there, and they'd curse his cheek. Dan couldn't see that it mattered, as long as his mother got the food.

He was very tired by the time he got back to Rosebank, hid the bicycle, climbed the drainpipe, and let himself in through Juanita's window.

He found to his dismay that the little warm room was empty. Then he cursed himself for an absentminded fool. It was her turn for night duty. Of course it was. What with various preoccupations, he had forgotten the Rosebank duty roster. He missed her terribly, her little firm friendly body and her sweetness and intelligence. He missed the bath which her absence made impossible. He missed food. He terribly missed food.

He could easily have bought a cake or a flan or a bag of pasties—anything ready to eat—while he was shopping for his mother. And he hadn't thought. He was famished, gnawed and distraught with hunger.

He wondered about risking a light. The curtains were pretty skimpy. It was highly unlikely there was anybody outside, looking at the house, knowing which Juanita's window was, knowing she was on night duty, knowing that a light in her room was odd and suspicious. But it was not impossible. The conscientious Stephen, the gentle-voiced and rubbery orderly, might do a last round out of doors, or might be coming back from a pub or a cinema. . . . The risk was not worth taking.

Dan knew the room well enough. He undressed in the

112

dark. When he was down to his underpants, his hand brushed something on the dressing table. It felt like an upturned plate. He groped for his trousers and found a match box. He lit a match, shielding the flame from the window, trying to fight down an enormous, unreasonable hope.

Under the upturned plate was another, and on the other two-thirds of a sort of open tart, pastry, egg stuff, bits of bacon and onion.

From his days at the bank, from little pretentious dinners in foreign restaurants, Dan remembered the word "quiche." Juanita had brought him two-thirds of a quiche. And a jug of water, so he needn't make the hazardous journey to the bathroom. And a knife and fork, so he wouldn't be covered in eggy custard.

Dan passionately wished Juanita had been there, so he could thank her immediately and immoderately. Meanwhile, it would be graceless not to take advantage of all her trouble. He wolfed the whole of the quiche, with two stiff whisky-and-waters. He licked plate and knife and fork completely clean (something his mother would never have permitted at home, but which seemed to him both sensible and polite). He sighed with gratitude and content, and went to bed and to sleep.

Juanita had one of her busier and more complicated nights. Mrs. Parker was convinced that her nephew Cedric was coming to take her to London in a taxi, and she wanted to be dressed and ready in the hall. Colonel Forbes wanted his lunch at three in the morning. He, Mr. Plante and Mr. Fortescue all wanted Matron to sit with them. She would have done so, Juanita knew, a time with each, but as it happened Matron was out, a dinner party, one of her rare evening engagements, all dressed up, driven by Stephen in the elderly Ford, the single Rosebank car. When Juanita had time to think, she hoped Matron was enjoying her evening, but what with Mrs. Parker and the old gentleman she had very little time to think about Matron, or even to think about Dan.

She trotted upstairs, exhausted, when she was relieved by Mrs. Mendoza at seven in the morning. She took her breakfast up with her—an exceptionally large breakfast. She and Dan shared cup and cereal bowl and plate. They shared footsteps along the creaking passage. Dan shaved and brushed his teeth under cover of the noise of the bath running. They shared the bath. Juanita was off duty until mid-afternoon. They shared her bed.

Juanita slept until noon, in Dan's arms. Dan slept part of the time, gazed affectionately at Juanita's face on his shoulder part of the time, and most of the time tried to make the rest of his plans for Saturday morning. He went through the name of every man he knew, looking for the right witness to have by him in the Priory Woods. He considered the whole of Medwell Fratrorum—nobs, tradesmen, village people; farmers and carters and keepers in the area; bank officials and professional men he had known in his days in the bank; even policemen. The requirements were so simple. Someone he trusted; someone who trusted him; someone the police would believe.

He concluded in despair that there was no such person in the world.

Juanita woke up, yawned, stretched, grinned at him,

snuggled up to him, her firm little breasts prodding his chest and her fingers busy.

She took his mind off his troubles.

Later her head on his chest, she said, "I've been thinking about the future."

"So have I," said Dan.

"Short-term and mid-term and long-term."

"I've been concentrating on the short-term, mostly."

"I can see how you might. I've been thinking about mid and long. You've changed everything for me."

"Oh," said Dan, suddenly full of apprehension and compassion.

"You've given me back myself. I came here and hid. Went to sleep. Hibernated. Frightened to poke my nose out. You've woken me up. Of course I approve of this place and I know it's loving and caring and worthwhile, but . . . I don't think I'm *very* hard and selfish."

"I don't think you are," said Dan. "I agree. You must get out and get on with your life. But it's tricky. As tricky for you as for me."

"I don't really know how I stand. I'll see a lawyer. I might go back to university. Anyway I'll re-emerge. Not today or tomorrow."

"Good," said Dan.

"Not until you're fixed up. And then . . ."

"And then?"

"Do you know Etherege?"

"There's a bloke with a name like that who keeps the pub in Little Barnington. Oh no—he's Elleridge. Tom Elleridge. A horrible bloke. False hearty with an R.A.F. tie. How do you know Tom Elleridge?"

115

"The man I mean is Sir George Etherege. A Restoration poet. He died of drink. I studied him last year. He wrote a poem to a girl called Cloris. Most of them did."

"Were there lots of girls called Cloris?" asked Dan. "Or one who got around a lot?"

"I think it was just a poetical name, like Lucasta and Anthea and Althea and so forth . . ."

"I never knew a Lucasta," said Dan. "I never did meet one of them."

"Etherege finishes like this," said Juanita, turning her head to face Dan solemnly:

> *"Cloris, at worst you'll in the end*
> *But change your lover for a friend."*

"That's nice," said Dan, thinking about it. "Yes, that's good."

"That's me. You. Us. Not yet."

" 'At worst'," quoted Dan.

"At worst, at best. This is lovely, heavenly, but it's something we're stealing. I've got to come back to life and you've got to look after your mother and your dogs and so on. . . . So one day we'll kiss goodbye and change a lover for a friend."

"For life."

"Yes, of course, for life. I'm very lucky and happy to have you as a lover, and all my life I'll be very lucky to have you as a friend."

Dan hugged her, moved, pleased.

He thought of Peggy Bowman, far back in his past as lover but still a good friend. He thought of Libby Franklin at the riding school, rather achingly recent as lover and certainly lifelong friend.

Juanita dozed off again—she had only slept for four

hours and she had had a long and exhausting night. She was very comfortable in Dan's arms.

Dan grinned to himself with affection and gratitude at the thought of Juanita, at the thought of Libby. They were in almost comic contrast—Juanita black as a chimney flue, Libby with hair so fair it was almost white. Juanita was far better educated and more sophisticated. Libby was probably more self-possessed. In all important ways they had a lot in common—both honest, affectionate, generous, sweet, really lovable. Juanita would always be his friend, as Libby would always be his friend. Libby was away at the moment, sent by the old Misses Hadfield to study dressage so she could teach it to the pupils of the riding school. . . .

And suddenly Dan had solved his problem.

Once again Juanita had done it for him.

By accident, but it was a nice irony that she'd mentioned that poet, that poem, so that he wouldn't worry about her feelings. It was typical of her. It had made him think of Libby, rather disloyally at that moment, with Juanita naked in his arms, but maybe that was typical too. And thinking of Libby had solved his problem for him.

Dan couldn't leave Rosebank by daylight, by the door or the drainpipe. He decided to stay the night and leave in the dawn. Juanita approved of this decision.

She brought him more leftovers from the staff dining room. She thought Stephen might have seen her carry a plate of cold beef upstairs. But there was no expression on his smooth pale face. Anyway there was no rule against having a midnight snack.

* * *

117

Through a chilly dawn, in a banker's suit becoming hourly more disreputable, Dan bicycled to Albany Farm.

The early frosts, amid the brilliance of the late summer, had painted the hedgerows with a brilliance of reds and russets and golds which was almost vulgar. The leaves of the field maples looked as though they were on fire. There was something, to Dan's sleepy morning eye, almost un-English about such extravagance of garish colour. As his pedals brushed the uncut verges of the lanes, his trouser cuffs became encrusted with burdock burrs and the little clinging seeds of goose grass, each plant taking every means to distribute its progeny far and wide, and seizing on Dan's trousers, with little barbed spines, as transport for the next generation.

Dan was content to play stork for infant weeds.

The frost had withered away the long lush grass in the wayside ditches, revealing a mist of seedlings sowed by the early-flowering plants. Many would survive the winter, and in the spring there would be regiments of tall purple foxgloves, and into their dangling bells bumblebees would stuff their corpulent hairy bodies, with a noise like a tiny power saw. . . . Dan wondered if he would be free to see it. It seemed long odds against.

Albany Farm, in a lazy loop of the river, was almost an island. Dan had known the place all his life, and the obstinate old ladies who owned it. Miss Trixie Hadfield, Miss Hettie Hadfield, daughters of a Colonel who had bought the place, for solitude and horses, after the First World War. The daughters had carried on exactly where the Colonel had left off, spiky, snobbish, unsociable, quarrelling constantly between themselves but offering a granite united front against the world, teaching the children of local tradesmen to ride the fat old ponies. . . .

And taking selected groups out hunting in the early autumn.

The old ladies were already up when Dan scrambled off the bicycle by the redbrick farmhouse. They had to be. With Libby away they were doing all the work themselves—bringing some ponies in, putting others out, feeding and watering and grooming and mucking out, manhandling bales of hay and half-hundredweight sacks of horse nuts and oats and bran and sugar beet.

Miss Trixie was wearing breeches, gumboots, a tweed coat, a man's shirt and tie, and a large red beret that gave her the air of a midget paratrooper. There were straws in her straggling grey hair. There was a great deal of muck on her boots. Her face was weather-beaten and deeply lined, and she had a voice like a corncrake.

She came out of the open half-door of a loose box, with a large horse dropping, nested in straw like something packaged for Easter, balanced on the tines of a pitchford. She stood holding this offering over a waiting wheelbarrow as she stared at Dan with bright, suspicious eyes.

"What do you want here, young Mallett?" she said. "Scrounging or stealing?"

To Miss Trixie, nothing had ever changed (except the world, for the worse) and nothing ever would. Dan was still to her, after twenty years, the undersized schoolboy who had helped in the stables in return for some riding.

"Runnen for me life, ma'm," said Dan.

"Yes of course. Some policemen came here yesterday to

ask if we'd seen you. Damned time-wasting interfering jackanapes, and so we told them. They said you'd killed somebody's gameskeeper."

"They ben putten 'at about," admitted Dan.

The Misses Hadfield, though grotesque, were genuine nobs, like Admiral Jenkyn and Dr. Smith and Matron at the Rosebank Nursing Home, not false nobs like Major March and Sir George Simpson. For this reason it was probably unnecessary for Dan to adopt, when talking to them, the treacly parody of rural Wessex which went down so well with the ignorant transplanted townies. But habit held. If Miss Trixie had heard him use his bank-manager's voice, she would simply not have believed the evidence of her senses.

"I always knew you'd die on the gallows, young Mallett," said Miss Trixie, unaware of the abolition of the death penalty. She would, of course, ignore anything of which she so contemptuously disapproved. Her father, in India, had carried out several executions with his own hand.

She finally dropped the forkful of manure in the wheelbarrow, where it slapped heavily onto the odorous coffee-brown porridge already there. A few droplets of mulch, flung outwards by the impact, lodged on Miss Trixie's jacket and in her hair.

Dan Mallett began to tell her exactly what had happened, omitting Peggy Bowman's name, though not her crucial role in the course of events leading to Edgar Bland's death. He tried to keep the story simple, not because Miss Trixie was simple—she was as sharp as a scythe blade, as sharp as his own mother—but to preserve the useful image of his own innocent simplicity.

Halfway through the story Miss Hettie joined them, leading two woolly, mud-crusted ponies in from one of the paddocks. She was not quite as old as Miss Trixie, but she was still very old. She was dressed identically to her sister, except that her beret was green. She was a miniature marine commando, with wispy gray hair and a smear of mud on her cheek.

"Why haven't they arrested you yet, young Mallett?" she said. "Idle, incompetent jacks-in-office. None of us are safe in our beds."

Dan had to begin his story all over again, to the visible annoyance of Miss Trixie.

There was a silence when he finished, broken by Miss Hettie's sniff and by the restless movements of one of the ponies she was holding.

"We're cubbing on Saturday," Miss Trixie said at last.

"Be ye taken a passel o' childer, ma'am?"

"Three or four. We can't take more, with Libby away. They get overexcited. The ponies hot up. Last Saturday the Master was . . . outspoken, when little Gwennie Barnes was carted and nearly trod on a hound. Hound's fault. Idle animal. Should have been hard at work in covert, not skulking outside. I gave it a tickle of whipcord. Master didn't like that either. But if the Second Whip isn't doing his job, the field have to do it for him. I was hunting before he was sitting on his pottie, and so I told him."

"Children have sharp eyes," said Miss Hettie unexpectedly.

Dan nodded. And old ladies—these old ladies—had sharp eyes too.

Cub hunting could be pretty boring, unless you were

on foot with hounds in the covert, and knew their names and their breeding, and understood what they were trying to do. Otherwise you were apt to sit for an hour on a horse at the edge of a wood, while invisible things went on inside. Dan knew. He had come out with the Misses Hadfield, as a young schoolboy, times without number. The old ladies would be glad of an additional diversion. Something, too, to keep their pupils amused. On this basis, it seemed to Dan, they agreed to his request.

He had no idea whether they believed his story.

Dan was amused, but not surprised, that the police had asked for him at Albany. His association with the place was well known.

His association with Libby was not well known. He burgled her cottage, at the far end of the property, at the top of the loop of the river. He spent a thoughtful day in warmth and comfort. He could have got a key from the Misses Hadfield. But he did not want them doing sums in their funny old heads about Libby and himself, because it would lower their opinion of Libby. He was a scrubby peasant, and she was the manager and chief instructor of their riding school.

Also he did not want the old ladies in trouble for harboring a fugitive from justice.

He knew Libby would be happy for him to use her cottage, and eat what food he could find.

He was uncomfortable with all the memories which thronged the cottage, of love and violence, and joy and terror, and Libby knocking him out with a poker. . . .

He thought about Saturday morning and about Juanita.

* * *

Juanita asked Matron for leave on Saturday morning, so that she could see what she had so often heard and read about but never seen—a pack of English foxhounds.

Matron seemed surprised that Juanita wanted to do something so hearty and traditional as follow hounds on foot, and surprised that she had heard about the meet and knew where and when it was. Juanita, bad at lying, invented something.

Matron had to refuse Juanita leave. Rosebank was short-handed with the illness of a nurse and the departure of two cleaning ladies.

It occurred to Juanita afterwards that Matron might be deeply opposed to blood sports. Juanita took—had taken—no sides in the matter. People she knew at Bristol University had formed hunt saboteur gangs, and gone out with trumpets and aerosols and furious convictions. Against that influence stood Dan. He knew much more about everything than they did, and he was her lover and her friend.

Juanita had got past being amazed at the spectacle of herself sheltering and feeding and sleeping with a man on the run from the police. She divided her life into two epochs: B.D. and A.D., Before Dan and After Dan. She felt a little shiver at her blasphemy, she the adopted daughter of a clergyman's household. But she did not think God—any God she cared to believe in—would mind so very much about the doings of a little black nurse and a little brown poacher.

In the daily papers which came to the staff dining room she read about the Medwell Court murder. There was a lot of lip smacking about a death by bow and arrow. The police wanted to interview a man. The papers made it sound as though there was no doubt whatever that Dan had done it, to resist arrest, to pay off an old grudge, and because he was the sort of person who killed people.

There were things Juanita did not know, but she knew very well that Dan had not killed anybody.

Meanwhile she was disappointed not to go cub hunting.

Dan kept out of sight of the meet, on the big gravel sweep in front of the Priory. There would not be many people there—nothing like the crowd when the season proper began—but many of those would know him. The hunt staff knew him, as he was sometimes an extra terrier-man and sometimes a midnight earth-stopper. The terriers and some of the hounds knew him. The little girls of the Priory school would be watching the meet from the gravel or the great windows of the house: some of them knew him, too, though they thought he was an officer of the secret service.

If Major March didn't come, on foot or mounted, with or without £1,000 in a plastic bag, nothing was lost except time.

It would have been best to go straight to the first covert, and pop up into Major March's view when he was sure the Major could be seen by the witnesses. But the wind was blowing fitfully in various directions, and there had been a lot of felling in the Priory Woods, changing the nature of the foxes' habitat, so Dan had no idea where hounds would be taken to draw first. He had to keep in touch and tag along with them.

He saw the hunt horses being unboxed and saddled, and reunited with the huntsman and the two whips. They were the only ones in scarlet—for cubbing, everyone else was in tweed ratcatcher and boots without colored tops.

124

Other people began to arrive, a dozen, twenty, cheerful, knowing or pretending to know, clattering up the Priory drive on horses that still needed exercise. The hounds arrived in their van, and spilled excitedly over the gravel, a mobile pattern of tan and white and blue mottle and badger pie, the young hounds puzzled but excited by the excitement of their elders. The whips were kept busy stopping the youngsters from straying. The Misses Hadfield arrived, in ancient greenish bowler hats, riding ancient ponies, and followed by four pink children on smaller ponies. Dan thought none of the ponies looked capable of carting even the smallest child.

A few cars arrived, with people in padded Husky coats and tweed caps and green gumboots. Bicycles arrived. The little girls swarmed out of the school and began kissing the hounds. Dan heard the huntsman shouting at the girls not to give sticky sweets to the hounds.

Major March arrived in his Mercedes. He was alone. He wore a Husky jacket, a tweed cap, and green gumboots. He carried a thumb stick and a pair of binoculars. He was dressed up as a countryman and a keen student of hound work. Actually, Dan thought, he was a keen student of dressing up as a countryman.

If he was carrying £1,000 in a plastic bag, he was keeping it hidden. Nor was he obviously displaying any gun, cosh or knife. The bulky padded jacket could be hiding a treasury and an armoury.

Another car came up just as the huntsman began to lead his hounds away. It was a nondescript car carrying three nondescript men. Two got out of the car and joined the foot followers. The driver stayed in the car. He looked cold and bored. There was nothing wrong about the two who trudged away with the rest after hounds, horses and bicycles. There was nothing quite right about them, either. One wore a deerstalker and a blue anorak and grey flannel trousers. These were not bizarre or unsuitable garments, but they looked odd in combination. The other wore a short grey mackintosh. He was bareheaded. This struck Dan as illogical. If he expected it to rain, why no hat? If he expected a dry day, why a raincoat?

It was not a large or important problem.

Both men were in their late twenties. Both wore their hair cut short; the one in the deerstalker had a neat gingery beard. Dan had never seen either of them. They were townies. They worked in a bank or in insurance or in an estate agency. They greeted people, but as strangers. They were interested in everything that was going on. Dan thought they might make useful additional witnesses, as long as they didn't alarm Major March.

Major March did not look alarmed. He did not look nearly as alarmed as Dan felt, as he prowled round the edge of the school playing fields on his way to being murdered by Major March.

9

DAN WAS unable to keep the whole proceedings in full view all the time. He was often unsighted by the straggling, scruffy undergrowth in the woods. Glancing down at himself, he saw that no skill or devotion of Juanita's could save what was left of his suit. His mother would be very angry. While he had it, she could indulge dreams that he would wear it regularly again.

The mounted field was fanning out, on the huntsman's instructions, a little back from the edge of the wood. Some of the foot people, who knew what was happening, also posted themselves as to fill the gaps between horses. When the proper season started, this would be a disastrous arrangement. The last thing anybody wanted was for a fox to be headed back after making a break out of covert. What they were hoping to do now was to let any adult fox get clear away, but turn the young ones back. Hounds might kill a brace or a leash of cubs without ever leaving the wood.

It was unfortunate that they were still called cubs, Dan thought—to city people that suggested cosy little puppy-like balls of fluff. In fact they were full grown by now—had been for weeks—and as greedy as old vixens. The

127

hunt's welcome among the farmers and cottagers depended on a good thinning out of the fox population, when the youngsters were still inexperienced and tied by their inexperience to their birthplaces.

Of course there was more to it than that. To Dan's knowledge there had been at least two litters in the Priory Woods, feeding mostly on rabbits. That was why he was careful to lock his bantams up at night, and to keep his fancy pigeons at the top of a ladder. There were no foxes in the Medwell Court woods—Edgar Bland had seen to that. What today's activities might do was to shift a few cubs out of an overcrowded covert into an empty one, spread the population more evenly, making for better sport later in the winter. They often ran straighter out of a strange covert, too—if they were chased out of their native place, they were apt to circle right back into it.

But what the huntsman was above all trying to do was to teach his young hounds, his new entry, to go to the cry of an experienced hound as soon as the latter spoke to the scent of a fox. There were hounds the rest of the pack trusted—hounds who never uttered except when they were truthfully saying they could smell a fox. Babblers who yapped with excitement or vanity, unsteady hounds who went after hares or roe deer, skirters who left the line of scent and let the others do the work—they had to be weeded out ruthlessly, or the whole pack learned bad habits.

Dan saw Major March—Husky, tweed cap, thumb stick, binoculars—rather close to the covert. Too close. A cub would be out and away before he could see it and head it. Too close if he was serious about the cub hunting. Not too close if he had other priorities.

128

The Misses Hadfield were sitting their ponies some twenty yards apart, with the four children posted between them and each side of them. They were close to Major March. They would remain so, Dan hoped, even if the huntsman posted them somewhere else. Dan didn't think he would. They knew what they were doing, they were loyal and lifelong subscribers, and they did not take kindly to orders.

One of the children was closest to Major March, a skinny little girl on a pony far from skinny. She was staring fixedly at Major March. She was making no attempt, no pretense, to watch the covert. Dan thought he had enlisted some pretty queer allies.

The hounds were deep in the covert now. The voice of the huntsman, on foot with them, filtered out through the trees and undergrowth, making those strange barbaric noises which generation taught generation, human and canine.

The mounted field began intermittently to whack boots or saddle-flaps with their whips. The idea was to frighten back into the covert any fox cub which had ideas about creeping away.

Major March looked intensely alert. He did not whack his boot with his stick. He was making no attempt to get out of sight. Presumably he was waiting for events to provide opportunities. He would be aware of Dan somewhere nearby, hiding and also waiting. The back of his head suggested a man aware of being watched.

Dan wondered what he was hiding under his bulky jacket—what weapons, what money.

A single hound came close to Dan, near the edge of the wood. It was a beauty, a baby, pure white, a Welsh-cross,

129

completely puzzled, probably unblooded, perhaps never having smelled the special acrid scent of fox, perhaps out for the very first time. It seemed disposed to turn to Dan for company and comfort.

A hound spoke, far away. The puppy twitched his rounded ears (unless they had been cut short in his babyhood, they would have been shredded by thorns and brambles) and quivered his stern in baffled excitement. Another hound confirmed. This was important. It eliminated guesswork. It was a fox. The volume of music grew, as fifteen or twenty couple of hounds sped to where the action was. The ancient noise excited Dan, as it always did, even though he was not in the wood to listen to hound music. The puppy bounded off, realizing that he was missing the fun. His serious education had that moment begun. Dan wished him well. He wished himself well, too.

Everybody outside the covert was still and attentive, watching and listening. Two of the children were standing up in their stirrups. Major March had come still nearer to the edge of the wood, to the sagging wire fence tacked to the trunks of the trees.

The two strangers—anorak and mackintosh—had separated. They could see each other. They were some way behind Major March, each side of him. There was something oddly symmetrical about their positioning. They were in perfectly correct, perfectly sensible places, if they wanted to see and to help. They made now—had made, as far as Dan knew—no contact with Major March. There was no reason they should stand where they could see Major March; there was no reason they should not do so. They might have been asked to stand just where they were standing by the Master or one of the whips. Dan thought not.

Dan was pinned down by the fact that Major March was in full view; Major March was pinned down by the fact that he was in full view. Neither could take any immediate action. Dan wondered if Major March was thinking, planning. Dan himself was using the time to think, though he did not attempt anymore detailed plan than the sketchy improvisation he had committed himself to.

Dan thought about the men in anorak and mackintosh, who seemed to be keeping a steady, unobtrusive eye on Major March.

They looked tough enough to be violent criminals. But too clean, too demure in dress and haircuts.

Neat young toughs with clean fingernails? Policemen. Detectives. It was screamingly obvious. Well, it was in fact far from certain. They might perfectly well be bank clerks, insurance salesmen, estate agents. Such people came hunting on foot. Dan had never heard of a detective doing so. But Dan thought these two were plainclothesmen brought in from another part of the county, unrecognizable to Major March.

They were watching the Major because they had grounds to think that he was going to try to kill somebody. Who? A blackmailer. Who else? They knew that he was being blackmailed. Or, to be more exact, they thought he thought he was. They thought he was a man who killed blackmailers. Someone was making more and better guesses about Edgar Bland's death, then.

Was any of this possible?

All that money Edgar Bland had been spending. It had added up to more than any bonus Major March would have been giving him. The police would have been to see Edgar's widow. Of course, spent hours there. Seen the awful cocktail cabinet and so forth. Asked questions and got a few answers.

Asked questions of Peggy Bowman?

Yes, certainly—she had given messages to Edgar Bland and taken messages from Edgar Bland on the last day of his life. She'd be a crucial part of any investigation.

The sight of Peggy—that bosom, that vitality, that obvious cheerful sexiness—would have given them ideas, unless they had very clean minds or very little experience.

Maybe it was from Peggy that they knew about Dan's blackmailing letter. She was the Major's confidential secretary, his bird. Maybe she knew what Major March was apt to try to do about it. She knew him pretty well. She could predict his reactions. She was no fool. She'd want to save Dan's life. Yes, thought Dan, considering the thing dispassionately, she'd probably want to save his life. She couldn't get in touch with him, warn him. He'd disappeared. So she went to the police. Yes, in a good cause she'd do that.

George Bowman was another who might come into the picture. Suspecting Peggy of frolics with her employer, and then building suspicion on suspicion, and then going to the police with the edifice. Perhaps Major March's dried-out old wife, the same kind of thing.

Dan pictured the police bombarded with suspicions, half clues, things too pat to be coincidence, all pointing in the same direction.

Dan decided to assume the two strangers were plain-clothes policemen there to watch Major March. As the morning wore on they would disappear. But they would still watch Major March. Major March himself would disappear, or try to. Dan would appear. What were the implications, for him, of this new complication? It was good if the police saw Major March trying to kill him, as long as they stopped the process. It was tricky but, yes, on balance it was good.

Dan was surprised to find himself welcoming the presence of two tough young bluebottles.

His thoughts were distracted by a glorious crash of hound music, and the horn blowing the kill. People would move now. Hounds and huntsmen would stay in this covert, surely, and the field would still be posted to ring it; but people would change places. Variety. Stare at a new tree trunk, a new clump of bramble. Dan got ready to move, waiting for Major March to move.

He did move, to his left, away from the Priory and the playing fields and the clump of mixed hazel and holly where Dan crouched. He moved slowly along the outside of the wood, two yards away from its decrepit boundary fence. He appeared to be strolling casually, with nothing on his mind and no particular objective. He glanced over his shoulder, then turned right round, still with an appearance of casual indifference, of mild curiosity. Quite near him he saw the Misses Hadfield and the four children, and the two strangers. From where he crouched, Dan had no idea how many more people Major March could see. Probably a dozen, but none near.

He was approaching the corner of the wood. It was almost a right angle, an unusual piece of geometry in a countryside where nearly everything was rounded or bent or askew. When Major March had rounded the corner, he would be invisible to all the people who could see him now, at least for a moment or two, even if the old ladies cantered to the corner. But the huntsman would have stationed people, mounted and on foot, along the next flank of the covert. Major March would come into their view. Dan wondered if he knew that—knew anything about how cub hunting was conducted.

But there was a track into the wood, starting just at the corner. A Land Rover or a tractor sometimes went in there, to take out dead stuff or a load of firewood. The track was deeply rutted, and brambles billowed out between the trees on either side, threatening to overgrow it. It was not used often. Dan visualized the track, remembering. It bent left after twenty yards, to avoid a patch of bog. The woods were undrained and full of boggy patches. When Major March had turned the bend, he would be completely invisible to anyone outside the wood, and hard to see for anyone in it, in his clothes of camouflage colour and in the denseness of the undergrowth. Dan doubted if Major March knew about the track. Why should he? But he was making for it as though he knew about it.

It occurred to Dan that the Major had reconnoitered the wood the day before. Military training. He looked like a man who knew exactly where he was going, although he was working hard at looking like a man who was not going anywhere.

Dan saw that he was pulling behind him, involuntarily, a sort of retinue. The Misses Hadfield and the four children, walking their ponies very slowly along the meadow beside the wood. The two strangers. All unhurried, casual, moving for the sake of moving. They were leaving the edge of the covert unguarded. A whole litter of cubs could get away. Major March could not get away, unless he went far down the track into the heart of the wood.

It was no longer possible to doubt that the strangers were there to watch Major March.

Dan was part of the retinue too, though he was invisible in the wood.

Major March was holding his head cocked a little on one side, the position of a man listening hard. Dan tried to move quietly, but it was impossible to be quite silent in a wood strewn with dead twigs and leaves. A snake—a centipede—would have made a noise. The hounds had another cub afoot and a dozen were giving tongue; they were crashing about in the covert fifty or eighty yards away; the huntsman was crashing about too and urging his hounds to kill more fox cubs. Dan thought hounds and huntsman between them were drowning the small crunches and rustles he made as he crawled through the undergrowth parallel to the edge of the wood.

Dan crawled further into the wood, towards the noise Major March, and the Misses Hadfield and the childen. They were all pretending not to be watching Major March, except the skinny little girl, who was still staring at him fixedly. But the strangers had disappeared. Dan was puzzled. What had seemed so obvious was no longer obvious.

Major March stopped, as Dan expected, by the mouth of the track. He stared down the track, as though hoping to see hounds and huntsman. He took another long, casual look around. He must have seen that the skinny little girl was staring at him with fixed, accusing intensity. Presumably he was not worried by the stares of little girls.

Dan crawled further into the wood, towards the noise

of the hunt. He neared the point he was aiming for, the bend in the track. He lay under a messy fallen willow tree, one of several in this boggy patch. He lay in boggy mud. The ground was cold and wet to the touch. He felt mud oozing between his fingers, and creeping up under the cuffs of his trousers; he felt muddy water beginning to seep through the stuff of his suit. The mud smelled of ancient decay. He lay as still as the rotting willow, at the edge of the track, camouflaged by mud and by dead leaves and brambles.

He could see to his left up the track to the edge of the wood and open ground. Ahead he could see down the track into the heart of the wood.

He saw a fox slip unhurriedly across the track. It was a big one—an adult dog-fox with a lot of white to his brush—the "holy water sprinkler" of the old days. The fox was not being hunted. He seemed to know it. He moved furtively but without panic. His situation was much more comfortable than Dan's.

Dan saw that Major March was walking slowly towards him, down the track towards the bend. He was no longer pretending to be casual, because no one could see his face. He was searching the wood as he walked, on both sides. He was listening intently. There would not be much he could hear over the noise of the hunt.

He would expect Dan to be doing exactly what Dan was doing—hiding and watching and waiting. He knew all about Dan, after Dan's trick on Edgar Bland. He knew Dan was a man who moved silently and close to the ground. He probably knew Dan badly wanted money— old Mrs. Mallett's condition was no secret in the village. He probably knew Dan would take considerable risks to get a thousand pounds in cash—would risk getting close to Major March, trusting in his nimbleness and woodcraft to get away. Major March would be trusting in the speed of his own reactions, the effectiveness of his own weapons, to stop Dan getting away.

What Major March didn't know was that he was being watched, and by a trustworthy independent witness. Near the mouth of the track Dan saw, fleetingly, the brim of a bowler hat. Miss Trixie or Miss Hettie Hadfield dismounted, creeping down the track after the Major. They had guts, those old ladies. Whichever one it was was probably making a fair amount of noise, not having had Dan's training or any need for it, but it was drowned by the other noises. An army could have got through the covert unheard.

Dan waited, his face and chest pressed into the stinking mud, motionless except for his eyes.

Major March stopped at the bend in the track. His boots were four feet from Dan's head. It was a bit too close. Dan was not in a position where he could jump up and run in one movement. He had to extricate himself from the mud and the fallen willow. Major March would reach out and grab him before he was clear. Dan wanted Major March to go on a yard or two down the track. Then Dan would show himself. He would run up the track towards its mouth. The old lady would see Major March trying to kill Dan. She would see a weapon. Then they were home. At least, they were if Dan got away. But with a start of two yards, in those woods, Dan backed himself to get away from a heavy-built middle-aged man.

It was working. It was all working.

Major March went on the two yards Dan wanted, down

137

the track beyond the bend. He stopped. He looked all round, slowly, carefully. He unbuttoned the front of his Husky jacket. He pulled something out. It was a bright plastic bag, a shopping bag from a supermarket. In it was something the size and shape of a brick, but much lighter. A packet of bank notes. Or something masquerading as a packet of bank notes. Cheese, baiting the trap Major March was setting for Dan, not knowing that this time the mouse had set a trap for the cat.

Major March hung the bag on the branch of an alder which stuck out over the track. He hung it five feet above the ground. The bag was red and white, screening the name of the supermarket, a piece of vulgar litter, a lure to bring Dan to the shambles.

Dan thought Major March would go a little way away from the bag. He might hide. He would go far enough away so that Dan would think he was safe to grab the bag and run. The plan was an excellent one except for one major mistake. The Major thought Dan was primarily after the money, when really he was after something quite different. This was the factor which would save Dan and cook the Major's goose.

Dan waited for Major March to move on a bit, and to take out whatever weapon he was going to have ready. To Dan's surprise, the Major buttoned up his Husky. His weapon was in his pocket, then. Sure enough, the Major's hands went into his trouser pockets. They emerged with cigarette case and lighter. The Major took out a cigarette and lit it.

He was still standing inches from where the bag hung. His chest was almost touching it. That was a funny thing to do. He could not possibly expect Dan to make a grab for the bag when he himself was on top of it. He *must* move.

He did. He turned and strode briskly away, up the track towards the open meadow. He was past Dan's hiding place before Dan had a chance to move. He was now the wrong side of Dan. If Dan showed himself now, and Major March chased him, they would go deep into the wood and out of anybody's sight and the Major could kill Dan in peace. A few foxhounds would give no useful evidence.

Dan cursed himself. There had been a moment—a fraction of a moment—when he could have jumped up and run. The moment was gone.

The Major slowed, looking to his left in the undergrowth. He smiled and touched the peak of his tweed cap. He strode on. He had passed the old lady, one of the old ladies. Of course he knew them. He was probably surprised to see her lurking in the wood. It did not seem to bother him. He might have thought she was there to relieve herself, in the tactful obscurity of the thicket. He might have thought there were things about cub hunting he didn't understand—that the old lady was performing some arcane task connected with chasing fox cubs.

He went on out into the open, without a backward glance. He left the red-and-white plastic bag unguarded, unattended, garishly visible to anyone inside the wood, completely invisible to anyone outside it. Completely invisible to himself.

Dan remained motionless, trying to understand what was going on.

Major March was not baiting any trap at all. He was paying blackmail. It fitted. Slowly, Dan conceded that it fitted. The Major had paid Edgar Bland, paid him quite a lot, before he killed him. That, no doubt, was because Edgar went on and on, because he got too greedy. Dan had been over-simple in considering the Major's pattern of behaviour. He did kill blackmailers, but not at once. He tried buying them off first. Dan would have to do the whole thing again, perhaps again and again. He might, incidentally, make quite a lot of money before the Major decided to kill him.

Major March was clear away, out of sight.

The plastic bag hung impertinently, five feet from the ground in the middle of the track.

There was no point in leaving a lot of money for a woodman to find, or one of the rich little girls of the Priory school.

The whole of Dan's life (at least since he left the bank, and in some ways even before that) had taught him to look before he leapt, and to leap, when he did, deftly and inconspicuously.

He looked now, long and intently, up the track to the edge of the wood, down the track into the middle of the wood, and, as far as he could from ground level and in the middle of fallen trees and undergrowth, all about him in the wood. The plastic bag was like a luminous poster, a visible scream. It was hard to believe that nobody could see it.

The hounds killed again, a long way away, somewhere near Dan's cottage. Dan wondered fleetingly what would happen if a fox went to ground in those parts, and they brought up terriers and spades. Dan's Current Account and his Deposit Account and often a piece of borrowed

140

silver on its way to the "Box of Delights" in Milchester. . . .

The huntsman blew the whooping toot that called his
hounds together and took them away to another covert. It
was supposed to give the field the same message, but a lot
of people were ignorant. Not the Misses Hadfield. They
knew well enough. They probably knew every bugle call,
too, from their childhood in cantonments in India.

Dan dragged his mind back from visions of the old
ladies as young girls in khaki-drill riding habits—placing
them, in his mind's undisciplined eye, far back into Kip-
ling's India.

Faded khaki, greyish, like the dust of the parade
ground where their father's regiment of lancers advanced
and wheeled at the trot—like that broad dead leaf on the
willow just beyond the plastic bag.

A broad leaf on a willow tree? Willow leaves were nar-
row and pointed. They went yellow in the early autumn,
then fell and blackened.

Was it a leaf? It moved. It was blown out of Dan's sight
by the wind. There was no wind here in the dense shelter
of the wood, a yard from the ground.

Dan lay with his cheek in malodorous mud, pondering
broad grey leaves moving in motionless air. Movement
meant agency—bird, animal, man. There were grey
birds, but that was no bird. It was not part of any animal.

It was a bit of a raincoat, a greyish raincoat, cuff or
collar or shoulder. One of the tough young strangers.
Hiding, watching the plastic bag, having moved well and
quietly and cleverly. Having known exactly where to
come, and why. The other must be near, the anorak. The

141

other side of the track. Dan's side. Within yards of Dan. They'd moved, as Dan had done, under cover of the noise of the hounds. He'd been patting himself on the back, for so cleverly choosing this rendezvous with Major March, for so cleverly using the commotion of the hunt to conceal his movements. An army could have crossed the covert unheard. An army did. Quite a big enough army for the battle in prospect.

The strangers were not watching Major March. They were on his side. They were working for him, or he for them. They were policemen. Major March had gone to the police with the blackmail note. That was what he did with blackmail notes. He didn't murder people. He didn't murder Edgar Bland. Edgar Bland had not been black-mailing him.

All the theories which had become certainties in Dan's mind crumbled to powder, like the old mortar between the bricks of his cottage: flowed into formless ooze, like the mud where his chin rested.

The Hadfields and the children were still, no doubt, faithfully watching Major March. They might as well be watching the Archbishop of Canterbury.

Dan had dug a pit for Major March, and Dan had walked into it. The mouse had flattered itself, with insane conceit, that it was trapping the cat. The cat was far away, safe, innocent. The cat's friends were very near, waiting to pounce.

Entirely aside from plastic bags and blackmail notes, they would arrest him for murdering Edgar Bland.

Dan wondered, feeling a little sick, what would have happened if the man in the grey mackintosh had hidden behind a maple, a sycamore, a chestnut, any tree with big leaves.

The hunt had moved right away. Dan could just hear the horn, its shrill yap muffled by the acres of damp woodland. There was very little birdsong—the seesaw of a great titmouse, the chuckle of a blackbird, the remoter piping of a solitary throstle. There was no other sound at all.

If Dan moved an eyelash, he would be in Milchester Gaol within minutes.

10

DAN FELT something like despair, an emotion strange to him. It was not so much his immediate predicament, though that was unpleasant in the last degree. He foresaw more police, tracker dogs, and all kinds of discourtesies. What was worse was his complete, blank ignorance about Edgar Bland's death. It was all to do again, including the thinking. He had thought himself into the ground, to no purpose whatsoever: and then chance had handed him what he thought was the full answer. Chance had handed him an answer, all right, which fitted all the facts and what he knew about all the people. But it was the wrong answer. It was a lovely answer, convenient and convincing, but it did not have that objection.

Fed up with thinking, Dan still forced himself to think.

Major March's actions today, and the presence of the coppers in the wood, could be explained only one way. The Major was a good citizen. He was cooperating with the police. He wanted a murderer caught and a blackmailer caught, and these things were more important to him than his own reputation. Dan looked for any other motive that the Major might have, any other explanation of the morning's doings. He could find none. There was none.

144

He tried to keep his theory alive, because he was fond of it, and not fond of Major March, and he preferred having any theory to having no theory, but it died in his arms. Edgar Bland's murderer was somewhere quite different and someone quite different, and Dan had not the smallest idea who or where or what to look for.

Meanwhile, as on the night of Edgar Bland's death, Dan thought he faced the choice between being arrested and dying of exposure. Being arrested remained unwelcome. The case against him for Edgar Bland's murder was not, in the event, getting weaker. He had supposed so, for a lovely moment, when he thought the strangers were watching Major March. He had been as wrong about that as about anything, which was saying a bucketful. If anything, today's events would have the effect of strengthening the case against Dan, at least in everybody's attitudes. It seemed like the same kind of person—a dirty murderer, a dirty blackmailer. The huge priority, the single salvation, lay where it had always laid. In finding out who really did kill Edgar.

How? Who? Where? Motive? Knowledge of Edgar's movements? Skill with crossbow?

Dan could ask none of these questions to any purpose until he got out of the wood. That called for a bit of thinking about, too.

There was a little movement of the topmost branches in the fitful breeze. But very little. There was a little demure piping from those few birds which nothing kept quiet. But very little. There was no other sound whatever.

The policemen were just as good at holding still as Dan was, and they seemed just as determined as he was to go on doing it. They were probably a good deal more comfortable. They might even regard this assignment as a cushy option, practically a day off, sitting in a nice wood looking at a nice plastic bag.

Dan hated stalemates, and he never remembered a mate staler.

Time crawled by. If it grew no colder it grew no warmer. The mud was as wet as ever, and smelled as vile. There was occasional sunshine, but none of it came anywhere near Dan.

The stalemate was broken in the last way, and by the last person, that Dan expected, Miss Trixie Hadfield came into the wood. Looking up the track to its mouth, Dan saw that the skinny little girl was holding two ponies.

"Dan Mallett!" shouted Miss Trixie. "Where are you, boy?"

Dan thought it best not to reply, but hope began to sing a little song in his breast.

"We kept an eye on that March fellow for you," shouted Miss Trixie. "Until he went off in his car. So there's no further purpose in us waiting about or in you waiting about."

Miss Trixie had by this time reached the bend in the track. She stopped, looked around, and shouted for Dan again. There was no movement from the policemen. Miss Trixie saw the plastic bag.

"Filthy litter," she said.

She stumped up to it, her riding boots squelching in the mud of the track. She pulled it down from the branch of alder. She did not look inside it. She did not bury it, or tuck it under a root—she would not have dreamed of simply transferring such odious litter from one place to another. She was public-spirited. She rolled up the bag, round its brick-shaped contents, and tucked it into the inside pocket of her tweed hacking jacket.

She would burn it when she got home. Dan wondered if it contained a thousand pounds in notes.

"Hey," called the policeman in the gray mackintosh, surfacing suddenly from the undergrowth.

Miss Trixie, Dan knew, disliked people shouting "hey" at her as much as she disliked anything, and she disliked many things very much indeed. She was impertinent and peremptory herself, but she made different rules for herself. The man in the gray mackintosh had made an error of judgement.

"Put that bag back where you found it," said the policeman.

"It's your disgusting litter, is it? I suppose so. Nothing more likely. I know your sort. You trample into decent countryside and leave your filthy garbage for honest people to clean up. Get back to the slums where you belong."

"We are police officers," said the man in the blue anorak, now surfacing from his hiding place. As Dan expected, he was on the opposite side of the track from his friend, very close to Dan.

"A likely story," said Miss Trixie. "Policemen don't hide in woods. I suppose you're some of those hunt saboteur scum. Rent-a-mob. It's all ignorance. Ignorance and intolerance. We don't interfere with your disgusting wrestling matches. If you knew anything about country life, you'd know that hunting with hounds is by far the most humane method of controlling foxes. The only humane method. I suppose you'd gas them or snare them or shoot and wound them, so they die after forty-eight hours of agony. No doubt that's what you prefer. That or so many foxes no farmer's wife could keep a single hen. I have no patience with people like you."

There were, perhaps, faults in Miss Trixie's argument;

147

she was quoting the slightly tendentious handouts of the British Field Sports Society. Dan knew very well that the only humane way of controlling foxes was to drown litters of newborn cubs, as though they were unwanted kittens or puppies or baby rabbits. Of course that was sad for the vixen.

This was no time for Dan to be debating the ethics of blood sports. But it was an excellent time for Miss Trixie to be doing so.

"You are trespassing," she told the policemen. "We are here as the guests of the landowner. What we are doing is legal as well as necessary. You are breaking the law. If there was a real policeman here I would put you in charge."

But the policemen produced identification.

"That's no good to me," said Miss Trixie. "I haven't got my reading glasses. Why on earth should you suppose I'd bring my reading glasses out hunting?"

She refused to return the plastic bag to the branch.

Under cover of all this, Dan was able to crawl out from his fallen willow, and emerge onto the track out of sight of the disputants. He trotted to the mouth of the track.

"Hullo," said the skinny little girl, who was holding Miss Trixie's pony as well as her own. "Didn't that fat man kill you?"

"No," said Dan seriously.

"Then we've wasted all morning," said the girl.

"I'm right sorry," said Dan humbly. Then he said, feeling a little treacherous, "Miss Hadfield asked me to take the pony."

"Which pony?"

"Her pony. This old Marigold."

"Why?"

"Urgent an' secret mission," said Dan. "Matter o' life an' death."

The skinny little girl was reluctant to abdicate her important role as pony holder for Miss Hadfield, also engaged in matters of life and death: although it was evident that, for the girl, there had not been nearly enough death. She clung to the reins with an expression at once suspicious and mulish. Dan did not want to use force. The little girl looked capable of very loud yells, and in a mood to relieve the monotony of the morning by using the full power of her lungs.

At least there was nobody about, outside the wood. There were two too many people inside it. They had not showed themselves at the bend in the track. It seemed likely that they would do so at any second, while this ridiculous argument dragged on. Dan was almost dancing with impatience. The little girl pleaded duty, boredom, and the fact that her own pony needed company, and would bolt without it. Dan knew this was untrue—he had known the child's fat pony all its life, and it was far too idle and sweet-tempered to bolt. But rational argument was no good in this situation.

It was vexing that his disappearance—his very necessary complete removal from this place—was stopped by a skinny little girl in patched jodhpurs.

"Please," said Dan, trying his smile on the girl.

His smile worked on most girls. It had no effect on this one. She clamped her little mouth shut over the braces on her teeth, and clung doggedly to Marigold's reins.

Dan was terribly disinclined to try to get away on foot. Being covered in mud, he would cause far less comment

149

on horseback. People on horseback were apt to be covered in mud, especially if they had been cub hunting. They were apt to have lost their hats. It was true that people did not as a rule go riding, let alone cub hunting, in dark, dapper banker's suits: but Dan's suit was hardly now recognizable for what it had once been.

Dan wanted the extra legs, too. He wanted to go far away from these policemen and other policemen. He was sure that, if nobody came to the bait in the red plastic bag, bloodhounds would be brought to the wood. They had good ones in Milchester and they loved using them. It was their form of cub hunting. They'd go and get something of his from the cottage—and old coat, a sock—annoying and frightening his mother. So the place for Dan to be was well clear of the ground, on a beast that would leave only its own scent when it travelled.

The little girl was obdurate. She was enjoying the argument. She was seldom, perhaps, in such a position of power—a position to grant or deny to a grown-up what the grown-up badly wanted. And Dan was in her bad books. He had cheated her out of the murder she wanted to watch.

"Miss Hadfield will want my pony, and make me walk home," she said.

This was by far the strongest argument she had yet used. Dan admitted the force of it. He could sympathise with that one. Miss Hadfield would jock the child off and make her walk.

"Not," he said, after a moment's thought, "if you ride along o' me."

"Where are you going?"

"Far an' fast."

"Tinkerbell can't go far or fast."

Tinkerbell was her pony. She was right.

Dan tried flattery. He said, "Truth is, I want a lead over some o' they fences."

Emotions chased each other visibly across the little girl's face. Dan thought that pride and suspicion dominated, and that pride might just be dominating suspicion.

The policeman in the blue anorak appeared at the bend in the track. He did not at once see Dan, who was half hidden behind Marigold and Tinkerbell, keeping watch over their broad quarters.

Miss Trixie Hadfield appeared. She was holding the red plastic bag. She was still arguing with the policeman. Since they were both talking at once it was impossible to hear what they were saying.

The policeman in the grey mackintosh appeared.

"Off we go," said Dan, jumping into the saddle of Miss Hadfield's pony.

The little girl at last dropped Marigold's reins, presumably realizing that she would be pulled out of her saddle if she didn't.

Miss Trixie and both policemen saw Dan at the same moment. They all shouted, still incoherently.

Dan managed to find his stirrups with his toes, and kicked old Marigold into a reluctant walk, a more reluctant trot, and a deeply reluctant canter. The little girl bounced along beside him, looking ready to give him a lead over Becher's Brook. They were pursued by shouts. The ponies were fresh, though probably a bit stiff after so much standing about, but Marigold had a whim to show this by bucking rather than by proceeding at speed along the edge of the wood.

151

Dan remembered that Miss Trixie had been carrying her hunting whip. He hoped she had not used it on the policemen. He could have done with it, to keep Marigold straight.

He tried to think as they bucketed along.

The best and quickest way out of the area was to go by the Priory itself, and along the drive to the road. But the policemen had left their mate in the forecourt of the Priory. Obviously he was still there, waiting to give them a lift, and Dan a lift, back to the Milchester Police Station. And he'd be in radio contact with the station. He might not be one of the many policemen who knew Dan by sight, but he sure enough had a description. A mud-covered hatless man, wearing shoes instead of riding boots, would look like a fugitive to one of those nasty-minded bluebottles.

Dan hauled Marigold's head to the right, and set off across the scrubby land beyond the Priory playing fields. There was a shriek from the skinny little girl. She thought this was the wrong way to go. Dan grinned at her, and struggled to overcome Marigold's reluctance to go in any direction except straight home.

He looked over his shoulder. Far behind, he saw the policemen running towards the Priory. The car. The radio. Roadblocks and such. Decription of his clothes and of the pony. Of the little girl and her pony. Did they think he had taken her prisoner? As a hostage? For ransom? For a free pass or a pardon?

They came to another belt of useless, boggy woodland. Dan knew every yard of it. There was a path, marked "Footpath Only" on signposts at both end. People used it in the spring to steal the lenten lilies and in the early summer to steal the bluebells, but it was not otherwise attractive. It was not where anybody wanted to go. Courting couples preferred other places. Even Dan himself, who had taken girls almost everywhere, had never taken one into that wood. In the winter the path was very muddy. The ponies might not like the mud. They would leave deep hoofprints that would not take a bloodhound to follow. The path was the least of the available evils.

Dan made for the opening of the path, intending to lead the way. The little girl popped in front of him. She was going to give him a lead through the terrors of the wood. Once in the wood, her pony kicked up lumps of mud into Dan's face. It made little difference to his face.

He thought that, if he ever got safe back to Rosebank, he would have to take two baths, one on his own before the one he shared with Juanita. And then he would have to think about setting better traps for better-chosen victims.

Stems of hazel, branches of willow and birch, had here and there collapsed over the path. The ponies could step over most of them, or push through them, or the riders could duck under them. One fallen willow-branch definitely needed jumping.

"Don't follow me too close," commanded Dan's pilot.

Dan nodded humbly.

The branch lay two feet above the path. Walls of brambles prevented it being bypassed. The take-off was muddy but not, Dan thought, hopelessly deep or slippery. The ground looked all right on the landing side.

Tinkerbell was a good jumping pony—had once, in his remote youth, won a rosette at a gymkhana. Dan well remembered the excitement. But today was not his jumping day. The little girl kicked him into his rolling center, made encouraging noises in a voice like a steam whistle, and rode him at the jump. He stopped dead, his knees inches from the branch. The little girl very nearly popped over the jump on her own, but saved herself with a double handful of Tinkerbell's mane.

Dan heard the noise of a motor, some kind of engine, some way outside the wood. It was a diesel. It was a tractor. It was on the scrubby acres they had crossed. It was coming closer.

The police had seen or guessed which way the ponies had gone. After briefing their friend with the radio, they had commandeered the tractor. They would block one end of the path with it. Someone meanwhile, summoned by the radio, would be rushing to block the other end. A car, with dogs. Perhaps the car which had brought the police to Medwell Priory, but more likely another, with the dogs from Milchester. There was no way Dan could ride through the wood except by the path—it was all bramble and bog. If he got off the pony and made a run for it on foot, the dogs would pick up his scent within seconds. The damp ground, in deep shade, would carry a scent that even a greyhound would smell; on every bit of the undergrowth he pushed through, Dan would leave microscopic droplets of the aromatic oil which all creatures give off all the time. Once the far end of the path was blocked, Dan's goose was cooked.

But nobody had got there yet, Dan thought. If the ponies pushed on now, at once, without a second's delay, they could surely get clear. Then they could go where cars couldn't follow.

The little girl continued to cram Tinkerbell at the inviting little jump. Tinkerbell continued mulish. Dan knew quite well that he could pop over the obstacle on Marigold, and that Tinkerbell, shown the way, would almost certainly follow, It was not the end of the world if Tinkerbell didn't follow—nobody was after the child. But even at such a moment Dan shrank from hurting the girl's feelings. She would be very upset indeed to fail, and to be seen to fail, and to need a lead over an innocuous jump. Years of helping the Misses Hadfield had made him deeply, painfully, familiar with the complex emotions of little girls on ponies. Besides, there was no room for Marigold to pass Tinkerbell, who was occupying the whole width of the path and a bit over.

The girl was scarlet in the face. Her expression was utterly determined.

Dan heard, far ahead, muffled by the damp woods, almost drowned by the desperate mutterings of the little girl and the squelching of Tinkerbell's hoofs in the path, the wail of a police siren.

The thudding of the diesel behind had stopped.

Both ends of the path were blocked—or would be, very, very soon.

Between them, Tinkerbell and his rider were comprehensively poaching the ground on the take-off side of the branch; it was becoming a quagmire. Tinkerbell liked it less and less. The girl's determination had reached the pitch of obsession. For the fiftieth time she pulled Tinkerbell's head round, trotted him back and away from the jump, pulled him round again to face the jump, and kicked him into a canter.

Dan thought they were going to do it. And if they did, they might just be in time. The far edge of the wood, the far mouth of the path, was two boggy fields of rough grazing from the nearest road, which ran between Medwell and Milchester. The policemen and their dogs would have to cross the fields, and find the mouth of the path. Dan thought the path was not at all obvious from any distance, since it was so overgrown and little used.

Tinkerbell thumped untidily towards the jump, his jockey kicking and beseeching. She was riding all right. She was giving the pony a slack rein, and keeping her weight far forward over his withers. She was giving him every chance. Yes, they were going to do it. . . . But Tinkerbell dug in his forefeet and skidded, and dropped his wicked old head between his knees. This time the child did "come out by the front door." She popped unhurriedly, almost in slow motion, over the pony's head. She fell not onto the branch, to Dan's intense relief, but plump into the poached and gluey mud on the take-off side. She kept hold of the reins. She was on her feet immediately, quite undamaged. Dan imagined that her expression was as grimly determined as ever, but that was really only guesswork, as her face was now plastered in mud.

Dan had an idea which would save the little girl's face, and, probably, get them both over the jump.

He said, "I do want a lead over that big jump, Miss, but I wonder if you'd do better on this pony."

The girl had a foot in Tinkerbell's stirrup and she was just about to scramble aboard him. She stopped. She stared at Dan and at Marigold.

Idiotically, incongruously, a line of poetry came into Dan's head, remembered from far-off dusty classrooms in the grammar school.

"All his men/Looked at each other with a wild surmise . . ."

The little girl looked at Dan and Marigold with a wild surmise.

156

She said, "I've never ridden that one."

"Always a first time."

"Miss Hadfield would kill me."

"Better 'n you killing Tinkerbell."

"Did you hear the siren?"

"Seems to me I might have heard a sort of a siren."

"Police."

"Could have ben a police car, yes."

"And the tractor behind us."

"Ah, you heard that?"

"Of course I did. Oh dear. It's my fault. They'll catch you in a minute. I should've thought about you, and all I thought about was getting Tinks over this tree. Give me your coat."

"*What?*"

"You're not much bigger than me. I must make it up to you, for being so selfish. Miss Partridge in Sunday school says we must always try to make it up to people, if we've been selfish pigs."

"Not a pig," said Dan.

"Yes, rather a pig."

She took off her hunting cap, and piled her hair into a knot on top of her head, and crammed her cap back on.

"If they're not too close," she said.

"I can't let you do it," said Dan. "I can't let you take such a risk."

"What risk? What law am I breaking by borrowing your coat and pushing my hair under my cap? It should have been there anyway. I should have been wearing a hair net. Miss Hadfield very nearly sent me home. Please get off Marigold and give me your coat."

"You're a great girl," said Dan. "You're my second favourite girl."

"Who's your favourite?"

"I'll tell you when we have more time."

Dan dismounted. He did not see any serious risk in the little girl's plan, which was now also his plan. He did see a chance of getting away. Just the one chance. There was no other. Nobody would shoot the girl. She would be in no trouble. She would come to no harm on Marigold who, though large for her, was a sensible and good-natured pony.

He looped his reins over his arm, and took the other arm out of the sleeve of his mud-crusted coat. Marigold nibbled at the collar of the coat, without vice. He shrugged out of the other sleeve. The air struck cold through his cotton shirt. He took Tinkerbell's reins, and the little girl put his coat on. Small as he was, it engulfed her. She folded back the cuffs. Her small, filthy hands poked out of the cuffs like spiders.

She was too small to mount Marigold unaided. Dan gave her a leg up; she swung into the plate like a professional.

"Ooh," she said. "I am a long way from the ground."

"You look great up there," said Dan. "Leathers are a mite long."

He took the stirrup leathers up about five holes, and his new friend said she felt comfortable. He mounted Tinkerbell. The little pony was well up to his weight, for a short distance. He did not expect to ride a long distance. He did not seriously, expect to be allowed to ride any distance, but he was taking the one chance he had.

"Am I really your second favourite girl?" she asked suddenly.

"Honour bright."

Dan thought that, under the mud, she was pleased.

158

He walked Tinkerbell twenty yards back from the branch. The girl followed, on Marigold. Marigold was perfectly quiet. She was quite happy to be carrying the girl. They both turned, Marigold in front.

"On you go," said Dan. "Badminton stuff."

"Wembley," said the girl. "I'm scared."

"You'll be fine."

In the oversized coat, she looked much bigger than she was. At least, it was possible that she would from a distance.

She kicked Marigold rather tentatively. Marigold trotted towards the jump. The girl tried to get into a canter, but Marigold knew what she was doing. In boggy woods, she was much better jumping from a trot. She went lumping calmly up to the branch, steadied herself, got her hocks well under her belly, and fairly sailed over the branch. It was a much bigger jump than was necessary, and a much bigger one than the rider had expected. The rider squealed, and clung to Marigold's luxurious mane. She kept her seat. She squealed again, in triumph. Dan popped over the branch after her, also from a trot, standing none of Tinkerbell's nonsense.

Marigold did begin to canter, and went licking down the path. Dan was further camouflaged by clods of mud from in front. He shouted to the little girl to duck under the branches. She was all right; she was lying along Marigold's neck. She still had a good handful of mane.

Dan reined in, to Tinkerbell's disgust. He wanted to see what they faced, long before they faced it. He trotted along the path, further and further behind Marigold and the girl. He turned a corner and saw, some way ahead, the mouth of the path.

There was no one there—no one obviously silhouetted

against the sky. There might be regiments of bluebottles each side, out of his sight, with squadrons of bloodhounds.

Marigold's bouncy canter was carrying her rapidly towards that point. Dan wondered if the girl could stop. She might not want to, but there would come a time when she wanted to. Dan was not at all sure he had done the right thing, even though he had done the only thing.

Marigold and the girl bounced out of the wood into the field on the far side. They swerved to their right, going immediately out of Dan's sight. There were shouts, male shouts, an unguessable number of voices. Near, too near. The whole ploy was a failure.

Dan wondered whether to go back, or forward, or stay where he was; he wondered how long his mother would survive life in an institution, after he had gone to prison.

11

DAN'S INSTINCT was to ride hell-for-leather to the mouth of the track to see what was happening—to help the girl if she needed help, and if he could catch her. A contrary instinct prevailed—go careful. If the girl got Marigold going, Tinkerbell would never catch her. If Marigold got herself going, nobody would catch her until she got bored with bolting. If, on the other hand, Marigold was on the bit and under control, there was nothing to worry about.

Dan thought he saw running figures, far away across the fields outside the wood. They were running from left to right, in the direction Marigold had taken. No one was visible near the mouth of the track. No dogs could be heard. They wouldn't bring out the dogs, if they thought their quarry was in full view.

Could they really think the little girl was Dan? Was that even remotely possible? Say the policemen there had never seen Dan. The description would have said what?—small and slight, wearing a dark coat; an up-to-date description, a report radio'd by the man in the car at Medwell Priory would say covered in mud and riding a fourteen-hand chestnut pony with such-and-such markings. From a distance it was difficult to judge the size of someone except in relation to someone else or to something of known size. Especially if the person was sitting down, as on a horse. It was equally difficult to judge the size of a horse, except in relation to a man of known size or another horse of known size. At a distance, travelling fast, Marigold and the girl could easily look like a bigger animal with a bigger jockey.

Dan was beginning to feel very cold, coatless, in a cotton shirt, with wet mud sticking to every part of him. It was one of the thousand things he could do nothing whatever about.

He trotted Tinkerbell towards the mouth of the path, then walked. Ten yards short of the mouth he dismounted. He looked and listened. There was plenty of activity in the distance, but there seemed to be none nearby. But policemen were sneaky.

Tinkerbell was restless. He missed his friend. He was unused to solitude. He wanted to rejoin Marigold.

Dan walked delicately to the edge of the wood. The undergrowth each side of the path was thinner, scrawnier. It still offered good cover, but he could get into it. He did not think he could get Tinkerbell into it, without a lot of trouble and a lot of noise. He led Tinkerbell to the mouth of the path. As he reached it, he got behind Tinkerbell, holding the reins, crouching a little. He looked out at the world over Tinkerbell's shoulder: out over the two fields between the wood and the road, and right the way Marigold had gone.

Another hunt was going on, much more vigorous than the foxhounds' cub hunting.

Marigold was already two fields away to the right. They had jumped two hedges and the girl was still aboard. They

162

were a long way off. As far as Dan could see, the girl's hair was still under her cap. They were bouncing along in a hack canter, looking perfectly under control. Four men, two in police uniform, were racing after the pony. One of the uniformed men was having a good deal of trouble with a thorn hedge.

Directly in front of Dan, two fields away, a police car and two motorcycles were parked in the road. Another police car was travelling at about twenty miles an hour, parallel to Marigold and overtaking her. The road bent to the right. Marigold's present course would take her to the road, to be intercepted by the police car. That was all right. Marigold was well used to traffic. She was bomb proof, as they said in advertisements for horses. She would not shy at the car, even if they blew the siren. The girl was in neither danger nor, Dan thought, trouble.

Dan was.

As he had guessed, a sneaky policeman had lurked near the mouth of the path. Maybe he was simply a lazy policeman, who had not fancied running half across Wessex. The first Dan knew about him was a shout of "Hey!" a few yards away to the left.

He had seen Tinkerbell's head, poking inquisitively out of the wood, looking for Marigold.

Dan had reckoned on riding Tinkerbell away, maybe back to the Misses Hadfields'. That plan had to be abandoned. He dropped Tinkerbell's reins on his neck. He wanted to give him a slap on the rump, but the noise would have given him away. He pushed instead. He pushed Tinkerbell out into the field. Then he dived like an eel into the undergrowth.

They thought that was Dan on Marigold. So where was

163

the little girl? Here was her pony, riderless. So she had fallen off in the wood. Dan had cruelly, selfishly, cynically, left her to bleed to death. Here was work for the police. A mission of mercy.

Almost before Dan thought he was adequately hidden, the nearby policeman had run up and taken Tinkerbell's head. He looked round wildly—he wanted help, someone to hold Tinkerbell while he ran up the path to look for the injured child. There was nobody near. They were all chasing after Marigold. He tied Tinkerbell's reins to a branch. He trotted up the path, calling, "Hullo? Hullo? Are you all right?"

He would go all the way along the path to where the tractor was. He would tell the men with the tractor that Dan was clear out of the wood and being chased by half the Milchester force. They would help to search the wood for the child.

Dan peeped out of his hiding place to see how the hunt had got on. It had finished. There were men with Marigold, who was standing still. Dan wished he could hear the conversation. All those men, and the men in the cars, would know by now that Dan was still in the wood. Whatever the girl said, he had to be still in the wood. But there was nothing they could do to get this immediately to the others. It was barely possible that a walkie-talkie had gone with the tractor, but only barely.

If Dan rode away now, immediately, on Tinkerbell, he would be seen. By people who would know it was him they were seeing. The only way he could go was Marigold's way, or straight down to the road, or back up the track. What he wanted was another little girl and another dark coat, to imitate him again.

It was all a question of timing, then. The men on the road would radio to the man at the Priory that Dan was still in the wood; he would get this to the men with the tractor, who would continue to block their end of the path and to watch their side of the wood. Meanwhile the dogs which were surely in one of the police cars would be brought up to the wood.

What Dan had to do was to hope to get to the tractor before the message did, and before the dogs were in the wood, and to hope to get there without being caught, and to hope the tractor was left unattended, and that it was one sort of tractor rather than another, and that the key was in it. All reasonable hopes, taken singly, but the odds against them all coming true . . .

It was worth a try. There was nothing else.

Dan had to go very quietly and very quickly. He had to go far too quickly to be properly quiet, if he was to reach the tractor before the message did and before the dogs reached him. He had to go far too quietly for speed, or they'd hear him and catch him in the middle of the wood. Disliking compromise, Dan compromised, and crawled moderately fast making a moderate amount of noise.

The one good thing about a situation otherwise detestable was that the men with the tractor—now, presumably, in the wood—thought Dan was far away. They thought they were looking for a little girl who had been thrown or dragged off her pony. They would not be quiet—far from it; they would not go far from the path.

The strip of wood seemed immeasurably broader to Dan, crawling, than when he had licked across it on a pony. And immeasurably thicker and boggier. The journey was interminable, detestable. Dan felt himself be-

165

coming caked with mud more thickly, more evil-smellingly, then ever before even in a life generously plastered with mud.

He remembered, fleetingly, that he had no other clothes unless he could burgle his own cottage. It was the least of his immediate problems.

He heard the men, well to his left, on or near the path. Two or three. If three, the tractor was presumably unattended. If only two . . .

He expected to hear the dogs, being brought across the fields to the wood. They must have been by his cottage, to sniff something that smelled of him. The dogs would not be in a hurry, not yet having met his scent on the ground. Of course, he would not hear them until they did meet his scent. Then, like foxhounds, they would speak to the line, to tell each other and the handlers what they had found. Any second Dan expected to hear the deep bay of the police bloodhounds.

He reached the edge of the wood with relief. He had conceived a passionate hatred for its sticky wetness and its clinging undergrowth, but he knew he had to be grateful to both.

The tractor blocking the mouth of the path was an old-ish, beat-up diesel with a weatherproof cab. That was good. There was nobody near it. That was good. It was started with an ignition key, like a car, and the key was in the dash. That was good.

Timing remained crucial and the future remained messy and obscure.

Two or more of the policemen were about seventy yards away in the wood, calling to each other and to the little girl. They were out of touch with their mates. They would not remain so for long.

Dan inspected what he could see of the ground between himself and the Priory. The police driver there would appear any minute. It was surprising that he had not already appeared. He was on his way—he must be.

Dan climbed into the seat of the tractor. There were large plastic windows in the sides of the canvas cab, and a small one in the back of it. They were splashed with mud and semiopaque. He was practically invisible, except from the front.

He peered through the plastic side window to his right, praying for a sight of the police driver from the Priory, but not too close a sight—a good distant sight. He was praying that the man appeared before the dogs got to the far end of the wood.

He saw the driver, running, three hundred yards away, with a flapping mackintosh.

He started the tractor's engine. It thudded wearily. He advanced the hand throttle, got the tractor moving, and turned it directly away from the wood. He straightened the wheels. He pushed the throttle to full speed, and immediately jumped off the tractor on the side away from the oncoming policeman. He wriggled back into the hateful asylum of the wood.

The police driver, knowing Dan was still in the wood, would think Dan was driving the tractor. What would the policemen in the wood think? That the little girl had gone off on the tractor. Crazy as that was, what else could they think? Until they were put wise by the driver.

When the driver saw and heard the tractor moving,

would he give chase at once, or first tell his mates it was Dan on the machine? Either way, pretty soon they'd all be chasing after the tractor.

The tractor's speed was not great over the broken fallow ground—Dan guessed twenty miles an hour. It was making a terrific racket, and bouncing on ancient ridge-and-furrow and over stunted bushes of gorse and thorn. The bounces altered its course, to the right and then to the left and then to the right again. Pretty soon something would stop it, a ditch or the stump of a tree. The policemen would rush up and surround it. By that time Dan would be—where? He couldn't plan that far ahead. He was in the minute-to-minute business. Something might turn up.

Something did.

Three policemen burst out of the wood together, grey mackintosh and anorak and the bloke who'd caught Tinkerbell. They shouted when they saw the tractor and all three set off after it. The driver from the Priory was racing along too, impeded by his flapping coat. Dan planned to get away by following along behind them, using what cover there was and going to ground when they found that the tractor was empty. It was a detestable thought. It meant more crawling—hundreds of yards of top-speed crawling. It was probably impossible.

Dan's second favourite girl trotted out of the wood, riding Marigold and leading Tinkerbell. She stopped as soon as she was clear of the trees, though Tinkerbell did not want to stop. She stared, with amazement evident even through the mud on her face, at the sight of four men running after a tractor.

"Hullo, beautiful," said Dan, emerging from his cover.

The girl gave a squeak of surprise and grinned.

"I thought that was you on the tractor," she said.

"That's what our friends think," said Dan.

"Yes. That was clever of you. But they won't think so for long. What will you do now?"

"Go creepy-crawly all up along behind them."

"They'll catch you."

"They might."

"After all our trouble. That's foul. You can't go back the other way, through the wood. I saw them getting some dogs out of a van." She added with relish, "Slavering bloodhounds."

"You'd best be off to give Miss Hadfield her pony back."

"No. I've just had a super idea."

"We could do with a few of those."

"Listen. When I was wearing your coat and riding Marigold, they thought I was you."

"Yes. One day I'll try to thank you properly."

"If *you're* wearing your coat and riding Marigold, they'll think it's *me*."

"Gum. They might. They truly might. Is my face as muddy as yours?"

"Your face is the muddiest in the whole world. In the whole universe. You can't have my jodhpurs but you can borrow my cap."

"You'll get in trouble, riding without a cap."

"I'll say I lost it in the wood."

"I'll faithfully return it."

"I don't mind if you don't. I want a new one."

She dismounted from Marigold, and peeled off Dan's mud-encrusted jacket. Dan was glad to resume the garment, tattered and filthy as it was. The girl gave him her

169

cap, which was far too small for him. He mounted Marigold.

"You'll come with me?" he said. "Just for company, you know."

"Of course not, silly. If they see me riding Tinkerbell they'll know it's not me riding Marigold."

"Oh yes. You're better at all this than I am."

"Yes, I know. Good-bye, then. Couldn't I be your favourite girl?"

"You're running it powerful close," said Dan. "Something like a dead heat."

Marigold seemed puzzled at going yet again along the path through the wood, and jumping yet again the fallen branch.

Everything hung now on where the policemen on the other side actually were. If they were near the wood, the deception was impossible. If they were a long way away, it was probably still impossible, but it was a chance.

At the far end of the path, Dan once again dismounted and peeped at the world over the pony's withers. Two police cars and the van for the dogs were now all together just beyond the bend in the road, near the point where they had intercepted Marigold and the little girl. Half a dozen men were advancing towards Dan, from that point, preceded by three dogs and their handlers.

Dan was awed to see the size of the force sent out to catch him. Of course they did think he was a murderer and a blackmailer.

He mounted Marigold and rode directly down towards the road. He tried to imitate the girl's straight-backed riding-school style of riding, while at the same time shrinking inside the coat. They might not, at this distance, notice that he wore dark trousers instead of khaki jodhpurs. At least his face was the right colour.

He glanced back. One of the policemen waved. He waved back. Politeness seemed to require it. And the girl would have waved back.

He jumped Marigold with no difficulty over the first hedge, and with great difficulty over the second. There was a gate onto the road. He got off and opened it. He trotted along the grass verge of the road away from the policemen.

It was highly necessary to get off the road, a road being a kind of prison and a kind of goldfish bowl. A police car might come along the road at any second, in either direction, and pass him at a distance of four feet. Or any other car, with somebody inside it who knew him or knew about him.

He also felt a kind of obligation about Marigold, who had to be got back to Miss Hadfield or to Albany Farm. Horses were supposed to find their own way home, but in Dan's experience they were apt to stop and talk to the first other horses they saw. Then even if Marigold wasn't stolen, the tack probably would be.

Dan left the road by the first track that led away from the Priory. By back lanes and a few fields he steered a zigzag course to Albany. He put Marigold, untacked, into a paddock with other ponies. Marigold immediately rolled and became as muddy as Dan and as his second favourite girl—his almost-dead-heating-for-favourite girl. Dan put the saddle and bridle away in the tack room, although they were also very dirty.

It was about one o'clock. Dan was hungry and exhausted. He had to walk from Albany to wherever he was

171

going. He had to find out who had killed Edgar Bland, and then think of a way to get the police to share the knowledge. He had absolutely no idea what to do, what to think, where to go.

Dan walked for a long, long way. He found an unattended car, unlocked, with the key in the dash. He decided he had walked enough. There was a risk, but he decided to take it.

The car was out of gas. That was why it had been left.

After more walking—much more walking—Dan borrowed a bicycle, and went carefully to Quimbury and to Rosebank. It was teatime. Prowling round the house, Dan peeped into the room where the TV was. Juanita in her crisp white cotton was handing round pieces of cake to the old, old ladies who sat looking dumbly, numbly, at the screen.

There was nobody in the garden, in the late afternoon, on this chilly October day. Dan risked the drainpipe. He decided to risk going to sleep in Juanita's room, although there was clearly a thin chance that someone other than Juanita might come in. He did not risk the bathroom, passionately though he wanted a very great deal of soap and hot water.

He took off his shoes and the shocking remnants of his suit. He spread Juanita's red plastic coat on the bed, to protect her sheets and pillow from the mud all over him. He lay down, and felt sleep surging over him like the bathwater he so badly wanted. He thought muzzily of the lonely, confused old men downstairs, who called Matron "Veronica" and muddled her with their wives. She let them, and she let them hold her hand and mumble their confidences.

But if, thought Dan, with the last waking flicker of his exhausted brain, each thought Matron was his wife, why did they call her "Veronica"? Had they all been married to ladies called Veronica?

The point was supremely unimportant. Dan did not let it keep him awake.

He woke up to find the light on, the curtains drawn, and Juanita undressing. He watched her with sleepy approval before she realised he was awake. When she was completely naked she looked at herself in the glass with an expression Dan could not read. Then she glanced towards him. He thought he knew what was going through her head.

He was amazed at his luck.

Then the events of the day—muddled, frightening, bitterly disillusioning—came flooding back into his mind. He groaned, not at the thought of the past, but at the thought of the future. He groaned at his blank ignorance and helplessness.

Juanita kissed him, and smoothed his unruly thatch of mousy hair, and asked him how the great day had gone.

"A muck-up," said Dan. "I was wonderfully certain about everything—"

"And?"

"I was wrong."

"That's happened to me," said Juanita. "Twice."

Dan told her everything, for the first time. There was no longer any need to be coy about suspicions which had proved so idiotic. He paid proper tribute to the skinny little girl.

"I'd like to meet her," said Juanita.

"Yes, you'd like her."

"I'm jealous of her."

"She's jealous of you. I don't deserve it."

"No, you don't, but now you must come and have a bath."

Dan almost forgot his miserable ignorance and impotence in the joy of that crowded and busy bathtub. He emerged cleaner than he had entered; he thought Juanita must have emerged dirtier than she had entered, because of the mud he had shed into the suds. She didn't seem to mind.

"Stephen's out," she said an hour later, after a nap after a miracle, as they lay in one another's arms in her bed.

"So?"

"So I can get you a better dinner."

"You're my dinner."

"I'm your appetiser. He drove Matron off somewhere in the car."

"Matron. Veronica."

Veronica. His subconscious had been busy about that oddity while he slept, and some mysterious retrieval system had produced the results of its work.

"Gum," he said. "I've suddenly understood."

12

JUANITA snuggled up to him. She did not understand what it was that he had understood, and he was by no means ready to tell her.

He lay thinking, refreshed by the bath, refreshed by the girl, much refreshed by the thought of dinner. His mind felt clear and efficient.

He hoped his new discovery was better than his previous discovery.

He examined it in the light of all the things he knew had happened, and all the things he thought must have happened. It did not stand up any better than the Major March theory, but it stood up just as well.

It was not such a nice theory, because the new murderer was not such a nasty man, but it might have the merit of truth. The other theory was very nice, but it did lack that advantage.

Edgar Bland had been a blackmailer. That part of the original theory remained as right as it had ever been. All the telephone calls were explained as well by the new theory as by the old one. Edgar Bland's presence in the wood was explained by the telephone calls, of course; and the murderer's presence in the wood was explained by

175

Edgar Bland's presence there. The old man had been sent there to be killed, because he had become too greedy. But not, unfortunately, by Major March.

How had Edgar Bland become a blackmailer? That was easy to explain on the old theory. It was less easy on the new. But not impossible. It might be something they'd never know. It might not matter. Edgar Bland was a prying old snooper, in a pheasant preserve and anywhere else.

It was all a great pity, in a way. Dan might easily have decided to go away and forget the whole business, but for two things. He was in a desperate jam himself, and only rubbing the bluebottles' noses in the truth would get him out of it. And he was cross at the blame being put on himself. He could see the point, but still it made him cross.

Juanita woke up, stretched like a sleepy puppy, and smiled.

Dan said, "Do many letters come here?"

"Quite a lot for Matron. Business things, I suppose. Practically none for any of the patients. Sometimes postcards. None for me, because nobody knows where I am."

"Do you see them, Matron's letters?"

"No."

"Where does the postman put them?"

"The usual place. Through the door. There's the usual kind of slit in the front door. You know, with a flap inside. They go into a box. It's always locked. Stephen has the key. He unlocks the box when the post comes, and takes the letters to Matron."

"Why all that?"

"Because otherwise the patients might get at the letters."

"Yes, of course. I should have thought of that. Hide them away like squirrels, or tear them up. I'd dearly like to see those letters. Just the outsides. Never mind the contents."

"Why?"

"Could that be arranged?"

"If you went to Matron's office after Stephen had put the post on her desk, and she wasn't there, and nobody saw you . . . No, it couldn't possibly be arranged. But I could go and look at the letters. I can't in the least understand why you want to see the address of this place on a lot of envelopes. You *know* the address."

"Testing a theory," Dan said.

Crisp in her morning uniform, happy, a little frightened, Juanita saw Matron safely away into Mr. Fortescue's room. He had been calling for her.

She had seen the postman while she was giving Mrs. Humble her breakfast. She had heard the letters rattle into the box, and the hinged flap bang down again to cover the opening.

Carrying trays back to the kitchen, she had seen Stephen unlock the box, glance quickly and incuriously at the envelopes, and take the bundle into Matron's office. Then Stephen had gone off to do something about the boiler.

The coast was clear. Juanita squeaked along the hall on the composition soles of her shoes. She slipped into Matron's sunny and friendly office—more like a sitting room than an office, with Stephen's paintings and the fresh flowers even at this time of the year.

The letters were in a neat pile on the desk. A very neat pile, of course, since Stephen had put them there.

What on earth did Dan expect to learn from the outsides of a bunch of business letters addressed to Matron?

There was no conceivable harm in looking at the letters. It might be odd, but no one would have any cause to be annoyed. Dan was not even curious about the insides of the letters. Only the envelopes. It was crazy. But he was not crazy.

Juanita turned over the letters. There were nine. Three were addressed to the Rosebank Nursing Home. One of these was the electricity bill and one looked like another bill. One was addressed to "The Matron." Probably an enquiry about a vacancy. There were plenty of those. Two were addressed to Matron by name, "Mrs. Carmody" and "Mrs. Veronica Carmody." Handwritten. Friends. It was odd to think of her as Mrs. Carmody in this place where she was always Matron. Juanita knew nothing about Mr. Carmody except that he was dead.

The remaining three letters were for other people. No doubt Stephen, or Matron herself, would hand them round later. Two were for Mrs. Fortescue and one for Mrs. Plante.

That was odd. Mr. Fortescue's wife and Mr. Plante's wife had both been dead for years.

Juanita turned over one of the letters for Mrs. Fortescue. It was a business letter. On the back of the envelope the name and address of the sender were printed. Did Dan want to know that? Why could he want to know it? Conscientiously, to please Dan in case he wanted this useless knowledge, Juanita tried to memorise the name of the firm. Rudkin and Stott, solicitors, an address in Blandworth. Blandworth? A market town, Juanita thought, thirty miles away. She had never been there, and never expected to go there. Maybe the Fortescues had lived there, and Rudkin and Stott were their lawyers.

No. Think, Juanita. If these people were the Fortescues' lawyers, they'd know Mrs. Fortescue was dead. They were other lawyers, who didn't know Mrs. Fortescue was dead, and had been given Rosebank as Mrs. Fortescue's address.

How sad. It might give poor old Mr. Fortescue a nasty shock, to get a letter addressed to his long-dead wife. Matron might decide not to give it to him, or at least to warn him first.

Juanita committed Rudkin and Stott, Blandworth, to memory. It was not difficult. If Dan wanted the address he could get it out of the telephone book.

The other letter to Mrs. Fortescue also had a typed envelope, but nothing to say where it came from. The postmark was London.

Two letters, in one morning, to a woman who had been dead for ten years. It was an amazing coincidence. Rather macabre. Was that what Dan had expected? How could he have expected anything so weird?

And Mrs. Plante. She had been dead even longer. Her envelope had a cellophane window in front, with her name and address showing through. Well, her name and this address showing through. The envelope came from the Royal Bank of Scotland. Juanita thought it was a dividend warrant. She had often seen such things in that prosperous household near Bristol. A dividend from a company in which Mrs. Plante had been a shareholder. No. Surely not. A company with a computer which had suffered a slight hiccup, and printed out Mr. Plante's sex wrong? Juanita had no idea if this was likely, or even possible.

Had Dan expected this too? How could he?

The door of the office opened suddenly. Juanita dropped the letters and jumped away from the desk. She felt as guilty and embarrassed as she had that awful afternoon when the Reverend Athelstan Jones came in to find her on the sofa with her blouse unbuttoned. . . .

Stephen came in. He stopped and looked at Juanita with his eyebrows raised.

"I was hoping to have a word with Matron," said Juanita, in a voice which sounded hideously false in her own ears. She began to talk too much, out of embarrassment. "It's a sort of personal matter," she gabbled, "to do with my, well, my status here. I don't mean here at Rosebank, I mean in Britain. Because I'm supposed to be here as a student, you see, and . . ."

She ran down miserably. Stephen stared at her. She could read no expression in that large, soft white face.

"Have you been reading those letters?" he suddenly asked in his high, womanish voice.

"Of course not. They're all sealed up."

"Looking at them?"

"No," said Juanita, unused to lying and bad at it.

"Then how do you know they're sealed up?"

"They've just come."

"You've looked at them all. My God, another one. You treacherous little bitch."

Juanita stared at him in utter amazement. She had never heard Stephen use such words before. She had never seen him angry before. He was very angry. His hands shook and his moon face worked.

"Are you doing this for someone else?" he asked softly.

"No!"

"On your own account, eh?"

"No! What account? What do you mean?"

180

"You're not well placed for this sort of caper," said Stephen. "You're hiding here. I know all about that. I know all about you. Nobody knows you're here. If you disappear, nobody will know you ever were here. The other staff will think you've just done a bunk, like that Irish wench a fortnight ago. The patients will hardly notice one way or another, poor old vestiges. Disposing of you will be perfectly easy, in the middle of the night, with the car. We won't have to hide the body. Nobody will know who you are. Nobody will connect you with this place. You'll just be another little immigrant who met the wrong client. They might guess about another Ripper. That's an idea. We'll fix you up so it looks as though a madman did you in. Now I'd better take you to your room and lock you in. I'll tidy up the pieces later on. Will you come quiet, or shall I knock you out and carry you up?"

Dan lay in bed waiting for his trousers to dry. Juanita had tried sponging them and finished by immersing them. They were hanging over the radiator in her room, clean though not smart, still damp. His jacket and shirt were on hangers, no longer dripping but far from dry. The worst of the mud had been scraped off his shoes. They were almost dry.

There was a chance that Juanita would never get to see the letters. There was a good chance that none of the letters he wanted would come in today's post.

In the quiet of that sad and hopeless house he heard footsteps on the stairs. The squeak of composition soles. Nurse's shoes. Juanita's shoes. Dan grinned on Juanita's pillow, thinking of her, thinking of breakfast, thinking of her news about the letters.

There were two sets of footsteps. Juanita and who?

There was something odd about the way they were walking. Dan wished he could see. The footsteps started along the passage towards Juanita's room.

Dan jumped out of bed. Naked, he shivered. He pulled trousers, jacket and shirt into the wardrobe and climbed in himself. It was a lousy hiding place, but it was better than the bed.

The footsteps did not come as far as Juanita's room. They stopped a few yards short of her door. Another door opened. Dan heard a squeak. It might have been pain or fright or simply astonishment. It might have been Juanita's voice. There was the sound of a slap, and of a body falling to the floor. There was a small scream. Dan thought it came from floor level. He thought it was Juanita's scream. The door slammed shut and Dan heard a key turn in the lock.

A single set of footsteps squeaked away along the passage and down the stairs.

Dan emerged from the wardrobe. He wrapped a towel round his waist, and very cautiously opened the door. He peeped out. The passage was empty. There was no sound from anywhere.

His bare feet cold on the linoleum, Dan tried the first door, the one next to Juanita's. He did not think it was right. The door opened into a bare, completely unfurnished room. The next door was locked. The key was not in the lock.

Dan whispered, "Juanita," to the keyhole.

"Yes," she said, inches away. She was at the keyhole too. She said, "Stephen found me looking at the letters. He's going to kill me tonight and dump my body with the car. I don't understand. I'm frightened. Help me."

182

"Yes. Anything funny about any of the letters?"

"Two for Mrs. Fortescue and one for Mrs. Plante. They're both dead."

"Ah. No wonder Stephen was cross. Can you open your window?"

"It's barred. That's why they put me in here. I suppose it was a child's room."

"The bars firm?"

"Yes, like rocks. I can't bend them or shift them at all."

"And this door's pretty solid. I could get an axe. An axe makes a lot of noise. Stephen has the key in his pocket. There it'll be all day. We'll think of something in a minute. Any indication where those letters came from?"

"One for Mrs. Fortescue from some lawyers."

"Ah."

"Rudkin and Stott. In Blandworth. And one from Scotland, the one for Mrs. Plante."

"Too far . . . Blandworth. Yes, that fits. Far enough to be safe. But not too far for me, I hope . . . Mrs. Plante, Mrs. Fortescue. Well well well. And I wonder how many more . . ."

"Dan, why does Stephen want to kill me?"

"We won't let him."

"How can you let me out without breaking down the door?"

"We'll think of something."

Dan tried to think of something. He failed. He had no tools of any kind, nothing that he could use as a tool unless he pulled Juanita's bed to bits. Even if he had had tools, he would not have dared make the shocking noise involved in this quietest of all houses in the world.

He shivered, pondering.

He had to get away, right away, and quickly, to make telephone calls and catch a murderer, but he had to look after Juanita. The trouble she was in was his doing. She had taken the risk entirely for him. Her situation was his responsibility.

Juanita told him there was no furniture in her prison. It was another completely bare room.

Dan decided that the only thing to do was to ambush Stephen when he came in the evening to kill Juanita—to knock him out and get the key from his pocket, or wait until he had unlocked the door . . . but that might be too late. The whole project filled Dan with gloom and dismay. Stephen might not come alone. He was not working alone. A strong possibility was that Dan would be killed as well as Juanita.

If only Juanita could be got out, and Dan could carry on with his tasks . . .

He went into the empty room, and felt all that he could reach of the wall between himself and Juanita. It was absolutely solid and surprisingly thick. He had not heard Juanita fall through the party walls, but through his door and the other, open door. With a muffled wooden mallet and a cold-chisel he could cut a hole through the wall big enough for Juanita to crawl through. It would take all day. No amount of muffling would hide the crash of chisel on brick. He had no chisel.

He opened the window of the empty room. He searched the garden with his eyes. There was no one about. He leaned as far out as he dared. The air was very cold on his bare chest and shoulders. He could see the bars on the next window, outside the glass. he saw that the bars were heavy, and sunk into the masonry surrounding the window. They had been there for a long time and they would be there for a long time.

The implication was simple, and depressing. Stephen had to be neutralised, and only then Juanita's door reduced with an axe. To neutralise Stephen, Dan needed mobility. Little as he wanted to, he had to leave Juanita.

He went back to the keyhole to tell her so.

Juanita gave what sounded like a sob. Dan heard her sniff. Her nose was like a little black button. Dan did not blame her for crying. He tried to encourage her. He said he would be back later to let her out, and then it wouldn't matter how much noise they made.

Juanita did not want Dan to leave her. She wanted him to stay, to protect her and to let her out of the room. But he knew he had to go.

Dan went back to Juanita's bedroom and put on his clothes. They were not dry. The trousers clung unpleasantly to his legs.

Stephen would be prowling, inside and out, alert and suspicious. He would be sure, rightly sure, that Juanita was an agent, somebody's tool. He would think she'd been sent to look at the letters for exactly the reason she had been sent to look at the letters. He'd think . . . Dan thought hard about what Stephen would think. He tried to think himself into Stephen's position, his predicament.

Some relative of one of the inmates suspected something. Conceivably some professional man, doctor or lawyer or banker or accountant or stockbroker. Or Edgar Bland, before his death, had told somebody what he'd found out. Anyway, somebody knew or guessed. Juanita had been bribed to do a bit of snooping. That's what Dan thought Stephen would think.

Therefore the suspicious outsider (so Stephen's mind would run) would be waiting for a telephone call or a visit from Juanita. Or he'd come to Rosebank, innocently on a visit to a patient, or on business, or delivering something, to hear what she'd found out. What names were on those envelopes. Stephen must think the outsider must approach or be approached. Juanita's knowledge was no use until it was shared—no value to the outsider, no danger to Stephen.

Stephen would think, must think: the outsider will be waiting, now, for a communication from Juanita, and when it doesn't come he'll get extra suspicious, and make haste to Rosebank to talk to her. Or he's planning to come here anyway. One way or the other, he'll come.

Stephen wouldn't know who to look for, among all the people who might come to Rosebank. But he'd back himself to make good guesses when anybody came.

He'd make a very good guess indeed if he saw a stranger leaving.

Watching for somebody coming was the same as watching for somebody leaving. Stephen would be watching, sure enough, all day and all night, with eyes at the back of his head and all round it. The faithful drainpipe and the expanse of bare garden were out of the question. Once on a drainpipe you were absolutely committed, absolutely helpless. You were a beautiful target.

The stairs and hall were out of the question. The drainpipe and garden were out of the question. Dan was as much a prisoner as Juanita, as long as Stephen was around.

Diversion. Dan must create a diversion, a catastrophe of the kind that, at Rosebank, only Stephen could deal

186

with. Serious enough so that he had to deal with it. A fire. An exploding boiler. Dan had nothing to start a big fire with, unless he went down into parts of the house he dared not approach until he had started a big fire in another part. He could probably find the boiler, but probably not without being seen. He had no idea how you exploded a boiler.

He thought fires and exploding boilers threatened the safety of helpless old patients to an unacceptable degree.

Any obvious diversion—shouting, running about, throwing things downstairs or out of windows—would simply reveal him to Stephen and surrender him to Stephen. All kinds of complicated manoeuvres—ghosts, thumps, booby traps—suggested themselves to him. He knew none of them would work.

And suddenly an idea came to him, after an absurdly, an unforgivably long time. It had been slow in coming simply because it was so simple. It was too childish to have suggested itself sooner.

Dan thought his almost-favourite girl would have had the idea at once.

He went along to the bathroom of happy memories. He jammed the plug firmly in the plug hole. He turned both taps of the bath full on. Then he turned the cold tap off. He decided steam was more valuable than speed. He took the key out of the bathroom door. He went out, closed the door, and locked it from the outside. Through the solid door he heard water from the hot tap thundering into the bath.

It would take time, which was bad. Nobody would get hurt, which was good. It would do a fair amount of damage, which was unavoidable.

Probably there were no locks at all on the bathrooms the patients used. There might be a duplicate key for an upstairs bathroom used only by the staff. It was doubtful. It looked like a day for axe work.

Dan waited in Juanita's room. He would rather have been crouched by the keyhole of her prison, talking to her. But that door was too far from safety, and Dan knew that Stephen could move quietly and guessed he could move quickly. Dan sat on Juanita's bed, with the door ajar, ready to bolt into the cupboard, listening to the rush of water into the bath just audible from down the passage. The note changed as the bath filled. It took a few minutes to fill. He could not hear the water slopping over the sides of the bath onto the linoleum of the floor. He saw, peeping through the crack of Juanita's door, a dark area beginning to spread from the bottom of the bathroom door. Water was seeping along the passage and beginning to trickle down the stairs. Somebody would notice pretty soon.

It was a long time before anybody noticed. Dan imagined plaster bulging above unconscious heads. He did not think ceilings would crash on ancient pates.

There were cries from somewhere. A coffee-coloured woman in a white overall ran upstairs and tried the door of the bathroom. She rattled it madly, apparently unable to accept that it was locked. She must have thought that someone had been running a bath and had passed out, fallen, fainted, died, drowned. That a confused old patient had somehow got up here and risked death by running a bath.

The woman dashed away. Obviously she was fetching Stephen. There was nobody else to fetch.

Tense, alarmed, Dan waited, squinting through the crack of the door.

Stephen ran soft-footed up the stairs. He would be highly reluctant to abandon his sentry duty, but the damage would be prodigious unless he stopped the flood. He carried a large bunch of keys on a piece of cord. He looked through the keyhole. Obviously he could see that there was no key in it. He tried keys, presumably on the off chance that some key he had on the bunch fitted the bathroom lock. From all points of view that was better than breaking down the door.

It was too soon for Dan to make his break.

Stephen ran away and down the stairs. Where did he keep his nearest axe? Outside in a shed? Dan was tempted to go. The prospect of meeting Stephen coming up the stairs was disagreeable. He held still.

Stephen still had no idea whether there was anyone in the bathroom or not. He must assume that there was.

Stephen ran back, not with an axe but with a kind of crowbar ending in a shallow, curved, slotted blade. It was a tool for raising floorboards, for opening locked bathroom doors. He inserted the blade just above the lock, and jemmied the door open. There was a large splintering noise as the lock, impaled in the door frame, wrenched itself out of the wood of the door. Steam engulfed him. Going into the bathroom, he would be unsighted, blinded by the steam. He would still not know if anybody was in there, some frail little figure huddled invisible in a corner.

Dan opened his door and went down the passage like a spider catching a train. As he reached the top of the stairs he heard the thunder of water cease.

He did not mind being seen now, by anybody but Stephen. Nobody else would be able to stop him, and nobody else would kill him.

Five women saw him, maybe more. He heard cries in various accents. He was out of the house before anybody touched him, and pelting away down the road.

He did not think any of the women would recognize him, even if they had seen Captain Cavendish.

13

DAN WALKED and trotted to Quimbury village, diving into the ditch whenever he heard a car. It was just possible that Stephen was out in his car. Once again, Dan got himself into a state where extra mud made no matter.

At the edge of the village, a woman looked at him oddly, and a child pointed. No wonder. Dan knew he must be a rum sight, with his damp and ruined banker's suit and mud all over his face.

He saw a woman come out of a cottage at the edge of the village. It was the cottage he had borrowed the bicycle from. He felt a little guilty at imposing on the same people twice, but he fought down his guilt. The woman was wheeling a small child in a pushchair. She was going shopping. Quite rightly she was not leaving the child in an empty house. Therefore the house *was* empty. She had a big basket and a smaller one on the handle of the pushchair. Extensive marketing, plus gossip. Dan guessed she'd be out of the house for an hour.

He saw two different wires running to the roof of the cottage, from two different sets of poles. Telephone as well as electricity. Dan blessed progress, which brought a telephone to a grubby little cottage on the edge of a remote village.

Dan got into the cottage through a little larder window which was closed but not fastened. A man of ordinary size would not have fitted through the opening. That was why the woman had not bothered to fasten it—probably never did bother. It was a squeeze, even for Dan. He left a lot of mud on the frame of the window. For the thousandth time he was grateful to small, flexible ancestors, who had bequeathed him the ability to crawl through larder windows.

He wanted to start by washing the mud off his face. But he started with the telephone. He looked up Rudkin and Stott in the directory. Fortunately Blandworth was in the same directory. He used his best banker's voice. He said that he understood that Rudkin and Stott included among their clients a Mrs. Fortescue, presently at the Rosebank Nursing Home in Quimbury. He asked to speak to someone who was concerned with Mrs. Fortescue's affairs and who knew her personally. The matter was urgent and confidential. The manner was as grand as Dan could make it. It involved the use of a special face, which he found necessary when he used a special voice.

He was put through to a Mr. Malcolm, a junior partner in the firm.

Dan said that he was Mr. Stephen Fortescue, a relative, though not a close one, of Mr. Fortescue. He said that there had been an accident and that Mrs. Fortescue, unable for the moment to come herself to the telephone, urgently required the services of her man of law. Would it be possible . . . ?

"Not this morning, Mr. Fortescue, I'm afraid," said Mr. Malcolm, who sounded too young to be even a junior partner. "Simply impossible."

"This afternoon? If not your goodself, Mr. Malcolm,

perhaps a clerk who knows Mrs. Fortescue personally, and can apprise you of her problem."

Dan had not used the word "goodself" since he had been taught to use it in business letters. He never had used it. It seemed to fit now.

He went on, more Fortescue than ever, "I cannot overstate the urgency of the matter, nor give you details over the telephone at this moment, as I am not alone and the matter is strictly confidential. I am sure you understand."

Mr. Malcolm said he understood, but he did not sound as if he did. This was not surprising, as Dan himself had no idea of what the crisis might be. He did not know if lawyers ever came out to clients in such circumstances, and at such short notice. It was very necessary that this one did.

It occurred to Dan to hint that, if Mr. Malcolm could not make it convenient to visit Mrs. Fortescue, another lawyer would be invited instead. Mrs. Fortescue's business would be removed from the hands of Messrs. Rudkin and Stott, and placed in more accommodating hands. Dan thought this ploy would work better with an old solicitor than with a young one, and with a big-city one better than with a small-town one. The successful and the metropolitan have less need for pride.

Mr. Malcolm promised in the end to come to Rosebank at four o'clock. He had never been there before. His meetings with Mrs. Fortescue had all been in his own office. This was exactly as Dan had expected. Thirty miles was an ideal distance.

Mr. Malcolm said he was fully aware of Mrs. Fortescue's circumstances, and could probably answer any questions she might wish to put to him.

"I understand her circumstances are pretty comfortable," said Dan carefully, "owing to the generosity of her husband."

Mr. Malcolm allowed that this was so.

Dan gave him directions for finding Rosebank from Quimbury village. He overflowed with gratitude and goodwill, expressed in banker's terms. He had to put on, while talking, a banker's face. He thought he must look and sound more incongruous than usual.

Dan was another three-quarters of an hour on the telephone. He found, in Ighampton, the bank where Mrs. Plante kept her account. The warmth with which the bank spoke of Mrs. Plante suggested that her account was sizeable, and comfortably in credit. Probably they had share certificates and insurance policies too. He found, in Barford St. Dominic, the bank where Mrs. Forbes had her account. One bank promised to send to Rosebank, at four in the afternoon, an assistant manager who knew Mrs. Plante personally and was conversant with her affairs. The other promised to send a senior clerk in the securities department who knew Mrs. Forbes. Both banks were highly reluctant to accede to the odd requests of, respectively, Mr. Stephen Plante and Mr. Stephen Forbes.

Dan would have preferred lawyers—anything to do with banks, even at long range, still gave him the cold sweats—but he could talk as banker to banker more convincingly. And there were far fewer banks in the area than solicitors. He only had to ring thirty before he struck lucky. The lawyers ran into hundreds, in the various towns of the district.

Dan telephoned Rosebank. He got the answering machine. He said that he was Major Stephens and he would visit Rosebank at four o'clock in the hope of making arrangements for the accommodation, at some future date, of his uncle, very elderly and somewhat confused, confined to a wheelchair, well able to pay for kindly private nursing. Major Stephens said he much hoped to meet the Matron, and would arrive at four in that hope. He could not be contacted in the meantime.

Dan thought Matron would be available at four o'clock. Major Stephens was the snare, the nylon monofilament noose to keep the quarry still while nemesis approached in a neat dark suit. Two bankers and a lawyer were gin traps, but they were no good without the snare.

Dan was laying his angles at Rosebank, as he had laid them at the edge of Cobb Wood.

He hoped Juanita would still be alive at four o'clock.

Dan saw the woman turn into the cottage gate with her pushchair. He departed by the larder window. He had still not washed his face. He thought that more than soap and water would be needed.

Dan was tempted to get a policeman or two to Rosebank, to join the party he was planning at four o'clock. He decided against any further telephone calls. He had been lucky. He did not believe in crowding his luck.

It would have been quite desirable to have a senior police officer as witness to whatever curious scenes were going to be played. But it was not really necessary. A lawyer and two bankers were surely witnesses enough.

There was another reason for not hanging about in Quimbury. Dan was eaten with anxiety about Juanita. He doubted if Stephen would murder Juanita in the middle of a bright afternoon, when an important visitor was expected. He wished this doubt could have been much, much stronger than it was.

Dan borrowed another bicycle, from a shed by another

cottage. It was a shocking old bone shaker, but it was better than walking in his ruined banker's shoes. He wasted a lot of time in the ditch, as harmless cars went by. It was highly unlikely that Stephen was out in the car, but it remained just possible.

In fact Stephen was at Rosebank, on guard. Peeping through the privet hedge, Dan saw the car parked by the front door. There was nobody in it or near it. There was nobody anywhere. As usual, the nursing home seemed absolutely deserted, silent, dead.

Indeed there might be death behind that gimcrack half-timbered facade.

There was no sign of life in the room where Juanita was. No scared black face at the window. She was sitting miserably on the floor, cold and lonely and frightened. Or . . .

Nobody at the nursing home had any idea about the visits they were going to receive at four o'clock. Though by now they would know about the visit they were not going to receive. They would be ready for a guest, but not for the guests they were getting. Dan wondered if Stephen linked "Major Stephens" with Juanita, with peeping at the names on envelopes. It must seem an obvious possibility that "Major Stephens" was somebody Edgar Bland had talked to. It was an equally obvious possibility that "Major Stephens" was the authentic relative of an authentic old gentleman. Stephen would be waiting with the most vivid curiosity for the arrival of "Major Stephens."

A nasty possibility was that one of the three professional men might telephone to change the appointment, or for some other reason. Crises did arise in offices. Dan remembered crises in the bank. They were his only enjoyable memories of the bank. If only one of the three had telephoned, the plan could still work—not so well, but well enough. But Stephen would be still more alert, suspicious, dangerous. The whole plan would be at risk and Juanita would be at risk. It would be a good idea for Dan to cut the telephone line to the house. He looked at the line, going to an insulator high on the wall above the front door, and at the pole from which it came. He abandoned the idea.

There was about an hour to go. Nothing would happen in that hour. Anything might happen.

Dan considered climbing into the house by his faithful drainpipe—making contact with Juanita, keeping an eye on her, comforting her if he could. And then somehow creeping to a seat in the stalls for the performance. But that drainpipe was still far too risky.

Dan tried to beam a message of comfort and courage to Juanita.

He tried to picture events at four o'clock. Expecting "Major Stephens," Stephen would find himself admitting the three actual arrivals. He would begin immediately smelling gigantic rats. Dan couldn't see that it mattered. He couldn't see what, by then, Stephen could do about it.

Suppose Stephen ran for it? There the car was. Dan decided to disable it. He wanted to take the make-and-break off the distributor, but he could hardly do that invisibly with the car parked where it was.

Dan crawled to the car, with his heart in his mouth, aware that he must be intermittently visible from some of the upper windows. He crawled under it. Groping, he found the valves of the two near-side wheels. He unscrewed the caps. With his fingernail he pressed the little pistons in the valves which worked the nonreturn system. Dan was vague about the technical terms, but he was

197

quite capable of letting the air out of a couple of tires. He went on until the tires were completely flat. Nobody would notice, coming out of the house and going straight to the car.

Stephen would still be on watch. He would be available when the visitor came. Therefore he would not go out in the car. Was that certain? Dan decided that it was certain enough. He reached up from below, opened the back door of the car very carefully, just enough to admit his snaky little body, and crawled in.

It was as near as he'd get to his seat in the stalls. It was a perfect place for watching the visitors arrive, and maybe seeing the reception they got.

He waited in the back of the car for three quarters of an hour, crouched on the floor behind the front seats. He saw and heard absolutely nothing. It was the longest forty-five minutes he had ever spent. Had it not been for the dashboard clock of the car, and the continuing brightness of the sky, he could not have believed that it was not a three-hour wait. There was nothing he could do but wait. He was tortured by worry for Juanita and by suspense.

A neat, new, small car drove into the front yard, and parked behind the Rosebank car. A man of about Dan's age got out. He wore a dark suit, neat black shoes, a white shirt and a dark tie; his hair was quite short and he carried a briefcase. He might have been a lawyer, but Dan thought he worked for a bank. Dan's heart went out to him in pity and contempt.

A nurse or maid unknown to Dan opened the door to his ring.

"Baines," said the newcomer. "Mendip Bank, Ighampton. To see Mrs. Plante."

Stephen appeared behind the girl. His manner was smooth. Nothing could be read in his face. If he was astonished or alarmed by this visit he showed no sign of it. He led Mr. Baines indoors and to Mrs. Plante.

Three minutes later a slightly larger and older car parked beside Mr. Baines'. It was another youngish man, but with a suggestion of tweediness. He might have been a doctor or an estate agent, but Dan was sure he was the lawyer.

He told the girl he was John Malcolm, of Rudkin and Stott, coming by appointment to see Mrs. Fortescue.

Stephen must have been doing large and rapid sums in his head, Dan thought, but he was bland and deferential to Mr. Malcolm.

"Mrs. Fortescue will be delighted to see you in just a minute, Mr. Malcolm. It is kind of you to come all the way out here. Who did you say made the appointment? A relation of Mr. Fortescue? But as far as we know . . . Well, well, no matter, will you take a seat in the hall here? Or there is an amusing programme on the television in the lounge. Several of the patients are enjoying it. For children, you know, at this time of day, but very well done. They get some wonderfully clever effects. I would love one day to see them making those cartoons. . . ."

Mr. Malcolm consented to wait a few minutes, with a fair grace. He followed Stephen indoors. Dan had no idea if he sat in the hall, or watched the children's cartoon on the television. Either way, he was not seeing Mrs. Fortescue at the same time as Mr. Baines was seeing Mrs. Plante.

Totally unprepared, Stephen was dealing superbly with a situation that should have filled him with despair.

The front door closed. Silence fell.

Mr. Baines and Mr. Malcolm were insulated from one another, by Stephen's adroitness. Even if they met, it would not worry Stephen, as long as their respective female clients were not present also.

Dan began to feel a cold lump of failure in his gut.

The third car came—another little new one. It parked by the new wing, in front of the Rosebank car but not blocking its exit. They were a terribly considerate lot.

It was another unmistakable bank official, young and scrubbed and keen-looking, Mr. Hubble from Bright's Bank in Barford St. Dominic, come by appointment to see Mrs. Forbes.

Any lingering doubt in Stephen's mind about what was happening must have been evaporated by Mr. Hubble.

But he said that Mrs. Forbes was certainly anxious to see Mr. Hubble again, and would be free to do so in a very few minutes. Mr. Hubble was offered a seat in the hall, by which Dan understood that Mr. Malcolm was watching television with the old women.

And all three would presently leave, in sequence, probably a little annoyed at the unimportance of the matters they had been brought so far to discuss, but putting that down to the whims of ladies of a certain age.

Dan realised what he had to do. He felt a little sick at the thought of doing it.

Stephen was certainly—almost certainly—hanging about in or near the hall, stage-managing the visits and the visitors. Dan had to get to the visitors. But not with Stephen there. Stephen would clobber him somehow, and have a story for the banker and the lawyer. After all, the place was a nursing home, and Dan did look unusual.

And no one in the world—not even Juanita, at this moment—knew where Dan was. There was nothing in the world, except Juanita, to link him with Rosebank. The body could be found or not found. It would make no difference to Stephen. He'd be safe.

Dan wondered if Stephen carried a key to the front door. He wondered if the door had bolts or chain, as well as the lock. He thought he remembered a chain, when Juanita let him in. He hoped he remembered correctly.

He had to hurry. Any minute the first visitor might emerge and drive away, unaware of the other visitors, unaware of anything amiss.

Stephen would be keeping an eye on the visitors, on the hall and the television room and the office. At least, Dan hoped he would.

Dan got out of the car and scuttled to the hedge. He broke a branch of privet out of the hedge. He went to the driver's door of the car, feeling miserably exposed, and switched on the ignition. He jammed the privet branch between the horn button and the back of the driver's seat. The horn blared throatily. The car was a bit decrepit but the horn was fine.

Almost before he had shut the car door, Dan was beside the front door, flat to the wall, his heart thudding, distinctly scared.

The door burst open. Stephen ran out. Dan ran in. He slammed the door on Stephen. There was a chain. Dan used it.

The horn stopped.

"Mr. Hubble!" Dan screamed. "Mrs. Forbes—oh quick!"

Mr. Hubble stood up so quickly that he knocked over

201

the chair he had been sitting on. He looked at Dan with his jaw sagging in amazement.

Dan heard Stephen trying the front door. He had a key. It was no good to him. Any second now he would run round to the back. He would know what was happening.

Dan dragged a reluctant Mr. Malcolm away from the television. He was enjoying an educational cartoon about penguins. Dan pushed Mr. Malcolm and Mr. Hubble into the sunny, civilized office where Matron twinkled through her gold-rimmed spectacles at visitors.

Mr. Baines, seated opposite to her, looked round at the invasion with a frown.

"Mrs. Fortescue!" said Mr. Malcolm.

"Mrs. Plante!" said Mr. Hubble.

Matron said nothing. Her face was grey.

Dan saw Stephen looking in through the window of the office. Stephen disappeared. Dan heard the self-starter, the engine, the horrible lurch of a car with two flat tyres.

Almost at once he heard another starter, another engine. Mr. Malcolm's and Mr. Baines' cars were in sight. Mr. Hubble's car had gone.

"I should have thought of that," said Dan.

Then he reached for the telephone, dialled 999, and for the first time in his life asked for the police.

14

DAN ASKED the lawyer and the bankers to keep an eye on Matron until the police came. They promised to do so. They were all still stupefied.

Dan ran to get an axe from the toolshed. He could not find Stephen's jemmy. He broke down the door into Juanita's prison. She was there. She was unhurt. She was cold and frightened and tearful. A good deal of the bathwater had seeped under the door of her prison.

Stephen had come to look at her. He had asked her questions she couldn't understand, and she had been too frightened to answer. He said he would have killed her at once, but they were expecting a visitor. He would kill her the moment the visitor had gone.

Dan blessed "Major Stephens," who had not only snared his birds but also saved Juanita's life.

He ran downstairs with one large problem still to be solved.

Faced with three professional men who knew her under three different names, Matron wept long and painfully. She blamed Stephen, through her sobs, for having the idea, for managing all the details, and for terrifying her into cooperating.

Dan introduced the name of Edgar Bland. Matron denied ever having heard of Edgar Bland. This was an understandable slip, in the confusion and horror of the moment.

"Edgar Bland ben a-visiten yere sen April," Dan told the others. "In course she knowed un. Any o' the staff yere 'll tell ye so."

Recovering a little of her fluttering and absentminded manner, Matron allowed that she had a sort of memory of someone called Edgar Bland.

"Edgar Bland were a-blackmailen she an' 'at Stephen," Dan explained. "Edgar ben an' tol' me. Said summat funny might come to un."

"That's a curious thing for a blackmailer to do," said Mr. Malcolm the lawyer. "Share his knowledge."

"Ah, but Edgar Bland were a lifelong friend o' me Dad. We'd come from same village, see, an' it'd mak' a bond."

"Withdrawals of substantial amounts of cash," said one banker to the other, "from your account or ours or a third. That will be easy to establish."

"Stephen arranged everything," said Matron, with unusual firmness.

"But ye signed th' cheques, ma'am," said Dan.

"As Stephen requested! He said the money was for— oh, how can I remember? For paint and so forth."

She was effectively admitting signing unusual cheques for cash. This was not lost on her listeners. She was very far from admitting that she had been paying blackmail.

"No jury 'll b'lieve 'at about paint," said Dan, still trying. "I seed what Edgar botten wi' 'at money. Thousands o' quids' worth o' fancy trimmens."

"I did as Stephen requested," said Matron. "I trusted him!"

204

"'At were a bloomer," said Dan. "'At Stephen, 'ere's a rat. 'Ere's a bloke clever enough t'disappear like a puff o' smoke in a gale. An' ye know what 'at means, ma'am."

Matron stared at him, blinking through her gold-rimmed spectacles.

An important moment had arrived.

Stephen was far too clever and careful to have left any clue by Cobb Wood. The police would have searched the ground with microscopes, and they would have found nothing to incriminate Stephen. That was certain. Stephen would have fixed himself an alibi. That was equally certain. Probably Matron herself. Probability might be built into moral certainty that a victim had murdered a blackmailer, but a good defense lawyer would make liver sausage of the prosecution case, as it stood now.

Which would leave Dan where he had always stood, the one with opportunity as well as motive, the one they knew had been on the spot.

Matron must be feeling betrayed by Stephen's desertion.

"Ye know what 'at means," Dan repeated, "'at Stephen runnen. Stephen ben an' lef' ye all alone, for t'go on trial for a-murderen pore Edgar Bland."

"I?" cried Matron. "No no! I could not possibly have done such a thing! I could not even pull that crossbow! I tried once! I was not nearly strong enough!"

Dan made sure that the lawyer and the bankers took this in, and would be able to repeat it to the police and to a jury. It did not add up to so very much. Not nearly as much as Dan had hoped. It was the rambling of a woman in extreme nervous tension. It was not a statement that Stephen owned or had ever used a crossbow.

The police arrived. Dan was immediately arrested for the murder of Edgar Bland. He was held at Rosebank pending the arrival of the detective chief superintendant, who was on his way. Meanwhile, the detective sergeant with a face like a Hereford bullock took preliminary statements from Matron, Mr. Malcolm, Mr. Baines, Mr. Hubble, Juanita, other members of the staff, and Dan.

Tenderly, tactfully, they extracted from Mr. Fortescue, Colonel Forbes and Mr. Plante that these old gentlemen believed themselves married to Matron.

Since the staff could not be taken away—to say nothing of the patients—the investigation had to be conducted on the spot. Dan was glad. He found the atmosphere of police stations inimical.

The police accepted, with amazement, the evidence of multiple identity, multiple bank accounts. They established from the staff the number of Edgar Bland's visits, and, by telephone to the banks, the size of the exceptional withdrawals in cash: the cheques having been signed by Mrs. Fortescue, Mrs. Forbes and Mrs. Plante.

Juanita told them that Stephen had promised to murder her, when he saw her with Matron's letters. This should have made it possible for the police to believe that Stephen had murdered Edgar Bland. But they did not seem to find it possible, because they were all perfectly convinced that Dan had murdered Edgar Bland. The fact that Dan had called the police to Rosebank had the effect of establishing, to the police, not his innocence but his impertinence.

Stephen was picked up near Milchester, trying to get petrol. The garage already had the make, colour and number of Mr. Hubble's car.

Faced with unanswerable evidence about the marriages, Stephen said that Matron had had the idea and had managed all the details. He himself simply did what he was told.

He admitted knowing Edgar Bland. He denied any suggestion of blackmail or murder.

He was questioned at Milchester Police Station. His statement was telephoned to the detective chief superintendant—the one who looked like a fox—who had just reached Rosebank.

During the ninety minutes of these events, the situation changed, but not enough. There was still, it seemed to Dan, a case against himself quite strong enough to bring to court. There was not yet, he thought, a case against Stephen anything like strong enough. The police were coming near to making bets with each other about which suspect would stand accused in the Crown Court at Milchester.

The patients had to be fed, regardless of police investigations. Juanita and the other staff were busy and bothered as usual, things worse because of the absence from duty of Matron and Stephen.

Matron was taken away in a police car. Dan expected to be taken with her. But he found himself still at Rosebank. He did not object to this arrangement. He found that, without anything being said, he was no longer under arrest. This change seemed to date from the superintendant's arrival. It was inexplicable, but Dan did not object to it, either.

The complex business of supper still eddied round the

house. Juanita looked exhausted after her ordeal, but she could not be spared from supper. Some of the policemen helped with the trays and trolleys.

Mr. Baines and Mr. Hubble left, the latter's car having been returned to him undamaged. Mr. Malcolm the solicitor lingered, out of professional and unprofessional curiosity.

"Why on earth didn't you come to tell us immediately how Edgar Bland was killed?" said the detective chief superintendant to Dan. "You would have saved yourself a lot of discomfort and us a lot of trouble. You would have saved that unfortunate suit of yours. The lads nearly had you on Saturday morning. We've been camping at your cottage, feeding your mother and looking after your damned menagerie. You were and are a pest."

"Putten me head in noose," said Dan.

"We would have arrested you, certainly. But only to put the murderer off his guard."

"The lads yere today thot I done un."

"Some of them, yes. The whole force isn't told everything. You were never suspected of murdering Bland. Every effort to catch you has been because we wanted your help."

"Niver suspecked . . ." said Dan, as utterly astonished as Mr. Malcolm had been two hours earlier.

"Of course not. From Bland's position when he fell, it was certain that he had been standing erect at the moment when he was hit by the arrow. He could not have fallen as he fell if he had been leaning or crouching. A crossbow is fired from the shoulder, exactly like a rifle. It has sights like a rifle. It cannot be fired accurately in any

208

other position. It was fired very accurately that night. When used at close range, the trajectory of the arrow is flat. The angle of entry of the arrow into the target thus provides an accurate measurement of the distance of the crossbow from the ground at the moment of firing. Provides, in other words, an estimate of the height of the firer accurate to within an inch or two."

"Gum," said Dan.

"Edgar Bland was killed by a man of approximately six foot one. Certainly not less than five-eleven. You are five-seven, I think?

"Thereabouts."

"Next time you're in trouble, for God's sake behave sensibly."

"Ay," said Dan humbly.

But trouble came in various forms, and he was not sure he saw sensible behaviour in the same light as the police.

"How on earth did they expect to get away with a succession of bigamous marriages?" said Mr. Malcolm to Dan and the superintendant.

"A-do guess," said Dan, clinging in this company to a modified version of his yokel role, "A-do b'lieves she never married *every* ol' man 'at were put yere by his fambly. There'd be a sight o' needs, like, for t'qualify a bloke t'be a bridegroom."

"Wealth."

"Ay. An' no lawyer a-managen the silver, wi' what they'd call power of attorney. An' no close fambly forever a-visiten. An' bed-ridden, or nex' kin to it, for 'at they didn't meet each other for t'compare notes, like. It must ha' ben a shock when ol' Plante went up thicky ladder. . . ."

"Then," said the superintendant, "in each new manifestation she'd take on a new lawyer, bank manager, stockbroker. The lawyer and the bank in the same town, probably, but a town she hadn't used before. It wouldn't matter if one of her lawyers met another, as long as not more than one met her at any one time."

"But handwriting? Signatures?" said Mr. Malcolm.

"Only Mrs. Fortescue's bank and stockbroker saw her signature, besides youself, Mr. Malcolm. They didn't see, and you didn't see, Mrs. Plante's signature or Mrs. Forbes' signature. You didn't hear their voices, either, however often you spoke to Mrs. Fortescue."

"Answeren machine were a sight o' security there," said Dan. "They never could be caught unawares by a bloke callen unexpected."

"But the registrar?" said Mr. Malcolm. "The marriages?"

"People from far away. A new one every time, of course."

"A-do guess ol' parsons from yere an' yonder," said Dan. "A-do b'lieves ye don't be needen a licence for a Church of England wedden. Jus' a parson, an' a bit o' paper after. It d'go in a book, an' all's legal. Then ol' husban, he d'start t'transfer stocks an' shares an' such, 'cause for he ben so grateful t'his loven wife."

"That must have been the pattern," said the superintendant. "Nobody else could have got away with it. Nobody else could even have tried it. It had to be a place like this, isolated, with patients of a particular kind, old and lonely and confused and fairly rich. . . . I wonder just how much those marriage certificates were worth to her."

"A-do wunner how many there ben," said Dan, awed. "How many a time she ben widowed. An' what were in all they wills."

"But," said Mr. Malcolm, still incredulous, still struggling against the logic of what he was hearing, "the men she married must have treated her differently, must have expected her to treat them differently—it must have been noticed. . . ."

"Nay," said Dan. "She did have a lovely line o' talk for t'cover 'at. She said the ol' gentlemen was forever muddlen her wi' their ol' dead wives. She let them, she did say. Why not, she did say, if it gi' un comfort. When ye saw an ol' gentleman callen Matron his wife, ye jus' chuckled, like, an' let be. A-do recall I were touched by 'at. Truly, she *were* nice t'them. Helded their ol' handies, an' let they rabbit on for hours, which were all they did crave."

"She was nice to them," said the superintendant "and by God she was paid for being nice to them. The next thing to do is to find out who's died here in the last ten years, and what became of their money."

"It's funny there's never been a will contested," said Mr. Malcolm, as though lamenting lost legal fees.

"Absence of close relatives would have been one of the desiderata," said the superintendant, "as Mallett here has pointed out."

"A-didn' put in so grand," said Dan humbly.

"And a very old man, without family, who's outlasted his friends, isn't visited. Except by some freakish circumstance, by someone like poor old Bland. Of course he found out. There's no doubt that explains his death. There might have been some doubt—" the superintendant

211

glanced at Dan, with a slight and unusual smile—"but not after what the Matron and Miss Jones have told us. But I wonder *how* Bland found out."

"Snoopen," said Dan. "He were forever at it."

"Will the woman be charged as accessory to the murder?" asked Mr. Malcolm.

"Oh yes," said the superintendant. "The man was obviously acting on her orders, in that as in everything else. I daresay he worshipped her, in some curious sexless way. It was a very ingenious murder. As near what thriller writers call a perfect crime as I've ever met."

Mr. Malcolm looked his curiosity.

"They telephoned Bland from here, to make that unusual evening appointment. The point of that was to leave the pheasant preserves unguarded that night. The fact that nobody knew the wood was to be unguarded, except Bland himself, his wife, Major March, and the secretary, was unimportant. What was important was that in Bland's mind his precious preserves were unguarded. They telephoned again to cancel the appointment. Perfectly reasonable and credible. They telephoned a third time, pretending to speak for Major March, saying that you, Mallett, were going to be in Cobb Wood. Obviously they knew your name from Bland himself. I gather he was obsessive on the subject. I understand he had reason to be."

"A mite o' cause," Dan admitted.

"It was a thing Bland talked about, in Medwell and everywhere else. Obviously he talked about it here, possibly to Stephen, possibly to Colonel Forbes and overheard by Stephen. Possibly even to the woman. So Bland thought you were going to be in the preserves, and he knew *you* thought he was going to be here. That made it absolutely sure that Bland was going to be in Cobb Wood in the small hours of that morning. Very neat. Really very neat. Economical and foolproof."

"An' it made sure I'd be blamed," said Dan. "Nasty trick, a-do call 'at."

"The fact that you really were in Cobb Wood was really neither here nor there, from the murderer's point of view. A bonus, but neither vital nor, of course, disastrous. But I wonder why Stephen didn't recognize you, when you came here pretending to be a client? He'd seen you in the full glare of a big flashlight."

"Ah," said Dan noncommittally. He was not anxious to explain his successful imitation of Captain Cavendish. The chameleon effect of accent and manner was not a thing to boast about to the police.

"But," said Mr. Malcolm, "I still don't understand how Bland did find out about those bigamous marriages."

"I suppose," said the superintendant, "his mind worked the same way as Mallett's did."

"But started from a diff'ent point," said Dan. "Edgar Bland were keeper to 'at Colonel Forbes long agone. He were hopen for a legacy. 'At be why he went a-ferreten t' banks an' such, asken a sight o' questions. 'At Matron did vow t'me 'at a lawyer were a-managen the silver, but 'at were a fib. She were a-managen. She were his wife, so the bank did b'lieve. Ye start wi' 'at guess, it on'y take a minnit wi' a phone t'put un all t'gether."

"Nobody did guess," said the superintendant. "Nobody else need ever have guessed. How did *you* guess?"

"Cam' t'me," said Dan modestly.

"Go on, man, before I borrow our friend's crossbow, which we found hidden in the garage."

"A-did see they ol' gentlemen a-treaten Matron like a wife," said Dan very slowly, as though shyly. "A-did b'lieve they did b'lieve she were so. She did explain 'at, right an' tight. But there were one thing right funny."

"*Go on.*"

"Ef ye was muddlen Matron wi' your wife, sir, how d'ye call her?"

"By my wife's name, of course."

"Ay. They all said 'Veronica.' Seemed to me they wasn' muddlen her wi' their wives. Leastways, a-disb'lieved three gentlemen in one house all had wives called Veronica."

"Good God. Was that all you had to go on?"

"Ay, till Juanita tol' me about they letters."

"And might have got herself killed. . . . She has nothing to worry about, by the way. The deputy chief constable has already spoken on her behalf to the Home Office. The infringement is technical, and she's clearly a desirable citizen."

"Ay," said Dan, wondering in what sense the superintendant was using the word "desirable."

"I imagine you'll both get a public congratulation from the trial judge."

"Nay!" said Dan in horror. "Not public!"

The superintendant laughed.

Mr. Malcolm grinned, but ruefully. He had valued Mrs. Fortescue's business.

* * *

214

Dan borrowed the Rosebank car, its tyres refilled with air, without actually asking anyone's permission to do so. He thought the police had enough on their minds.

He went to visit Miss Trixie Hadfield at Albany Farm. He wanted to make sure his second favourite girl was not in trouble with the old ladies for the episode of the ponies.

Miss Trixie brushed aside Dan's stammered and treacly explanations. She handed him a plastic bag from a supermarket. Inside it, something the shape of a brick rustled like dead leaves in a pheasant preserve.

"I understand that this is *your* litter, you incurable ragamuffin," said Miss Trixie. "The police asked me what I had done with it. I said I had burned it, as I burn everything in the incinerator. That has, I assume, been reported to that vulgar Major March. But why should I put myself to that trouble? It is your responsibility. I give it back to you in order to bring you to a sense of your duty. You must not foul the countryside with your mess. Take your rubbish and go."

"Did ye take a peek inside, ma'am?" asked Dan.

"I removed a few pounds for the hire of my pony for the morning. I think you will agree that is reasonable. Your mother needs the rest, for her operation."

Dan drove home and fed his bantams, pigeons, dogs and mother. His mother screamed at the state of his shoes and trousers, which he changed.

He drove the Rosebank car back to Rosebank. The staff were coping, though shocked and puzzled. A qualified nurse was being sent by the County Council in the morning, to take charge until a new permanent arrangement could be found.

The patients detected no change, though some of the old men called querulously for Veronica.

Juanita wanted a bath, though there was no lock on the bathroom door.

"You snared them," she said, "but I've snared you."

The lover, in Sir George Etherege's words, had not yet become a friend.

THE PERENNIAL LIBRARY MYSTERY SERIES

Delano Ames

CORPSE DIPLOMATIQUE   P 637, $2.84
"Sprightly and intelligent."

—*New York Herald Tribune Book Review*

FOR OLD CRIME'S SAKE   P 629, $2.84

MURDER, MAESTRO, PLEASE   P 630, $2.84
"If there is a more engaging couple in modern fiction than Jane and
Dagobert Brown, we have not met them."   —*Scotsman*

SHE SHALL HAVE MURDER   P 638, $2.84
"Combines the merit of both the English and American schools in the
new mystery. It's as breezy as the best of the American ones, and has
the sophistication and wit of any top-notch Britisher."

—*New York Herald Tribune Book Review*

E. C. Bentley

TRENT'S LAST CASE   P 440, $2.50
"One of the three best detective stories ever written."

—Agatha Christie

TRENT'S OWN CASE   P 516, $2.25
"I won't waste time saying that the plot is sound and the detection
satisfying. Trent has not altered a scrap and reappears with all his old
humor and charm."   —Dorothy L. Sayers

Gavin Black

A DRAGON FOR CHRISTMAS   P 473, $1.95
"Potent excitement!"   —*New York Herald Tribune*

THE EYES AROUND ME   P 485, $1.95
"I stayed up until all hours last night reading *The Eyes Around Me*,
which is something I do not do very often, but I was so intrigued by the
ingeniousness of Mr. Black's plotting and the witty way in which he spins
his mystery. I can only say that I enjoyed the book enormously."

—F. van Wyck Mason

YOU WANT TO DIE, JOHNNY?   P 472, $1.95
"Gavin Black doesn't just develop a pressure plot in suspense, he adds
uninfected wit, character, charm, and sharp knowledge of the Far East
to make rereading as keen as the first race-through."   —*Book Week*

Nicholas Blake

THE CORPSE IN THE SNOWMAN   P 427, $1.95
"If there is a distinction between the novel and the detective story (which
we do not admit), then this book deserves a high place in both catego-
ries."   —*The New York Times*

THE DREADFUL HOLLOW   P 493, $1.95
"Pace unhurried, characters excellent, reasoning solid."
                                              —*San Francisco Chronicle*

END OF CHAPTER   P 397, $1.95
". . . admirably solid . . . an adroit formal detective puzzle backed up
by firm characterization and a knowing picture of London publishing."
                                              —*The New York Times*

HEAD OF A TRAVELER   P 398, $2.25
"Another grade A detective story of the right old jigsaw persuasion."
                                              —*New York Herald Tribune Book Review*

MINUTE FOR MURDER   P 419, $1.95
"An outstanding mystery novel. Mr. Blake's writing is a delight in
itself."   —*The New York Times*

THE MORNING AFTER DEATH   P 520, $1.95
"One of Blake's best."
                                              —Rex Warner

A PENKNIFE IN MY HEART   P 521, $2.25
"Style brilliant . . . and suspenseful."   —*San Francisco Chronicle*

THE PRIVATE WOUND   P 531, $2.25
[Blake's] best novel in a dozen years. . . . An intensely penetrating study
of sexual passion. . . . A powerful story of murder and its aftermath."
                                              —Anthony Boucher, *The New York Times*

A QUESTION OF PROOF   P 494, $1.95
"The characters in this story are unusually well drawn, and the suspense
is well sustained."   —*The New York Times*

THE SAD VARIETY   P 495, $2.25
"It is a stunner. I read it instead of eating, instead of sleeping."
                                              —Dorothy Salisbury Davis

THERE'S TROUBLE BREWING   P 569, $3.37
"Nigel Strangeways is a puzzling mixture of simplicity and penetration,
but all the more real for that." —*The Times Literary Supplement*

Nicholas Blake (cont'd)

THOU SHELL OF DEATH   P 428, $1.95
"It has all the virtues of culture, intelligence and sensibility that the most exacting connoisseur could ask of detective fiction."
                    —*The Times* [London] *Literary Supplement*

THE WIDOW'S CRUISE   P 399, $2.25
"A stirring suspense. . . . The thrilling tale leaves nothing to be desired."
                                        —*Springfield Republican*

THE WORM OF DEATH   P 400, $2.25
"It [The Worm of Death] is one of Blake's very best—and his best is better than almost anyone's."   —Louis Untermeyer

John & Emery Bonett

A BANNER FOR PEGASUS   P 554, $2.40
"A gem! Beautifully plotted and set. . . . Not only is the murder adroit and deserved, and the detection competent, but the love story is charming."   —Jacques Barzun and Wendell Hertig Taylor

DEAD LION   P 563, $2.40
"A clever plot, authentic background and interesting characters highly recommended this one."   —*New Republic*

Christianna Brand

GREEN FOR DANGER   P 551, $2.50
"You have to reach for the greatest of Great Names (Christie, Carr, Queen . . .) to find Brand's rivals in the devious subtleties of the trade."
                                        —Anthony Boucher

TOUR DE FORCE   P 572, $2.40
"Complete with traps for the over-ingenious, a double-reverse surprise ending and a key clue planted so fairly and obviously that you completely overlook it. If that's your idea of perfect entertainment, then seize at once upon *Tour de Force.*"   —Anthony Boucher, *The New York Times*

James Byrom

OR BE HE DEAD   P 585, $2.84
"A very original tale . . . Well written and steadily entertaining."
    —Jacques Barzun & Wendell Hertig Taylor, *A Catalogue of Crime*

Henry Calvin

IT'S DIFFERENT ABROAD   P 640, $2.84
"What is remarkable and delightful, Mr. Calvin imparts a flavor of satire
to what he renovates and compels us to take straight."

—Jacques Barzun

Marjorie Carleton

VANISHED   P 559, $2.40
"Exceptional . . . a minor triumph."
 —Jacques Barzun and Wendell Hertig Taylor, *A Catalogue of Crime*

George Harmon Coxe

MURDER WITH PICTURES   P 527, $2.25
"[Coxe] has hit the bull's-eye with his first shot."

—*The New York Times*

Edmund Crispin

BURIED FOR PLEASURE   P 506, $2.50
"Absolute and unalloyed delight."

—Anthony Boucher, *The New York Times*

Lionel Davidson

THE MENORAH MEN   P 592, $2.84
"Of his fellow thriller writers, only John Le Carré shows the same
instinct for the viscera."   —*Chicago Tribune*

NIGHT OF WENCESLAS   P 595, $2.84
"A most ingenious thriller, so enriched with style, wit, and a sense of
serious comedy that it all but transcends its kind."

—*The New Yorker*

THE ROSE OF TIBET   P 593, $2.84
"I hadn't realized how much I missed the genuine Adventure story
. . . until I read *The Rose of Tibet*."   —Graham Greene

D. M. Devine

MY BROTHER'S KILLER   P 558, $2.40
"A most enjoyable crime story which I enjoyed reading down to the last
moment."   —Agatha Christie

Kenneth Fearing

THE BIG CLOCK   P 500, $1.95

"It will be some time before chill-hungry clients meet again so rare a compound of irony, satire, and icy-fingered narrative. *The Big Clock* is . . . a psychothriller you won't put down."   —*Weekly Book Review*

Andrew Garve

THE ASHES OF LODA   P 430, $1.50

"Garve . . . embellishes a fine fast adventure story with a more credible picture of the U.S.S.R. than is offered in most thrillers."
                                  —*The New York Times Book Review*

THE CUCKOO LINE AFFAIR   P 451, $1.95

". . . an agreeable and ingenious piece of work."   —*The New Yorker*

A HERO FOR LEANDA   P 429, $1.50

"One can trust Mr. Garve to put a fresh twist to any situation, and the ending is really a lovely surprise."   —*The Manchester Guardian*

MURDER THROUGH THE LOOKING GLASS   P 449, $1.95

". . . refreshingly out-of-the-way and enjoyable . . . highly recommended to all comers."   —*Saturday Review*

NO TEARS FOR HILDA   P 441, $1.95

"It starts fine and finishes finer. I got behind on breathing watching Max get not only his man but his woman, too."   —Rex Stout

THE RIDDLE OF SAMSON   P 450, $1.95

"The story is an excellent one, the people are quite likable, and the writing is superior."   —*Springfield Republican*

Michael Gilbert

BLOOD AND JUDGMENT   P 446, $1.95

"Gilbert readers need scarcely be told that the characters all come alive at first sight, and that his surpassing talent for narration enhances any plot. . . . Don't miss."   —*San Francisco Chronicle*

THE BODY OF A GIRL   P 459, $1.95

"Does what a good mystery should do: open up into all kinds of ramifications, with untold menace behind the action. At the end, there is a bang-up climax, and it is a pleasure to see how skilfully Gilbert wraps everything up."   —*The New York Times Book Review*

Michael Gilbert (cont'd)

THE DANGER WITHIN   P 448, $1.95
"Michael Gilbert has nicely combined some elements of the straight detective story with plenty of action, suspense, and adventure, to produce a superior thriller."   —*Saturday Review*

FEAR TO TREAD   P 458, $1.95
"Merits serious consideration as a work of art."
                                                       —*The New York Times*

Joe Gores

HAMMETT   P 631, $2.84
"Joe Gores at his very best. Terse, powerful writing—with the master, Dashiell Hammett, as the protagonist in a novel I think he would have been proud to call his own."   —Robert Ludlum

C. W. Grafton

BEYOND A REASONABLE DOUBT   P 519, $1.95
"A very ingenious tale of murder . . . a brilliant and gripping narrative."
                              —Jacques Barzun and Wendell Hertig Taylor

THE RAT BEGAN TO GNAW THE ROPE   P 639, $2.84
"Fast, humorous story with flashes of brilliance."
                                                       —*The New Yorker*

Edward Grierson

THE SECOND MAN   P 528, $2.25
"One of the best trial-testimony books to have come along in quite a while."   —*The New Yorker*

Bruce Hamilton

TOO MUCH OF WATER   P 635, $2.84
"A superb sea mystery. . . . The prose is excellent."
   —Jacques Barzun and Wendell Hertig Taylor, *A Catalogue of Crime*

Cyril Hare

DEATH IS NO SPORTSMAN   P 555, $2.40
"You will be thrilled because it succeeds in placing an ingenious story in a new and refreshing setting. . . . The identity of the murderer is really a surprise."   —*Daily Mirror*

Cyril Hare (cont'd)

DEATH WALKS THE WOODS P 556, $2.40

"Here is a fine formal detective story, with a technically brilliant solution demanding the attention of all connoisseurs of construction."

—Anthony Boucher, *The New York Times Book Review*

AN ENGLISH MURDER P 455, $2.50

"By a long shot, the best crime story I have read for a long time. Everything is traditional, but originality does not suffer. The setting is perfect. Full marks to Mr. Hare." —*Irish Press*

SUICIDE EXCEPTED P 636, $2.84

"Adroit in its manipulation . . . and distinguished by a plot-twister which I'll wager Christie wishes she'd thought of."

—*The New York Times*

TENANT FOR DEATH P 570, $2.84

"The way in which an air of probability is combined both with clear, terse narrative and with a good deal of subtle suburban atmosphere, proves the extreme skill of the writer." —*The Spectator*

TRAGEDY AT LAW P 522, $2.25

"An extremely urbane and well-written detective story."

—*The New York Times*

UNTIMELY DEATH P 514, $2.25

"The English detective story at its quiet best, meticulously underplayed, rich in perceivings of the droll human animal and ready at the last with a neat surprise which has been there all the while had we but wits to see it." —*New York Herald Tribune Book Review*

THE WIND BLOWS DEATH P 589, $2.84

"A plot compounded of musical knowledge, a Dickens allusion, and a subtle point in law is related with delightfully unobtrusive wit, warmth, and style." —*The New York Times*

WITH A BARE BODKIN P 523, $2.25

"One of the best detective stories published for a long time."

—*The Spectator*

Robert Harling

THE ENORMOUS SHADOW P 545, $2.50

"In some ways the best spy story of the modern period. . . . The writing is terse and vivid . . . the ending full of action . . . altogether first-rate."

—Jacques Barzun and Wendell Hertig Taylor, *A Catalogue of Crime*

Matthew Head

THE CABINDA AFFAIR   P 541, $2.25
"An absorbing whodunit and a distinguished novel of atmosphere."
—Anthony Boucher, *The New York Times*

THE CONGO VENUS   P 597, $2.84
"Terrific. The dialogue is just plain wonderful."
—*The Boston Globe*

MURDER AT THE FLEA CLUB   P 542, $2.50
"The true delight is in Head's style, its limpid ease combined with humor and an awesome precision of phrase." —*San Francisco Chronicle*

M. V. Heberden

ENGAGED TO MURDER   P 533, $2.25
"Smooth plotting." —*The New York Times*

James Hilton

WAS IT MURDER?   P 501, $1.95
"The story is well planned and well written."
—*The New York Times*

P. M. Hubbard

HIGH TIDE   P 571, $2.40
"A smooth elaboration of mounting horror and danger."
—*Library Journal*

Elspeth Huxley

THE AFRICAN POISON MURDERS   P 540, $2.25
"Obscure venom, manical mutilations, deadly bush fire, thrilling climax compose major opus.... Top-flight."
—*Saturday Review of Literature*

MURDER ON SAFARI   P 587, $2.84
"Right now we'd call Mrs. Huxley a dangerous rival to Agatha Christie." —*Books*

Francis Iles

BEFORE THE FACT   P 517, $2.50
"Not many 'serious' novelists have produced character studies to compare with Iles's internally terrifying portrait of the murderer in *Before the Fact,* his masterpiece and a work truly deserving the appellation of unique and beyond price."   —Howard Haycraft

MALICE AFORETHOUGHT   P 532, $1.95
"It is a long time since I have read anything so good as *Malice Aforethought,* with its cynical humour, acute criminology, plausible detail and rapid movement. It makes you hug yourself with pleasure."
                                    —H. C. Harwood, *Saturday Review*

Michael Innes

THE CASE OF THE JOURNEYING BOY   P 632, $3.12
"I could see no faults in it. There is no one to compare with him."
                                    —*Illustrated London News*

DEATH BY WATER   P 574, $2.40
"The amount of ironic social criticism and deft characterization of scenes and people would serve another author for six books."
                          —Jacques Barzun and Wendell Hertig Taylor

HARE SITTING UP   P 590, $2.84
"There is hardly anyone (in mysteries or mainstream) more exquisitely literate, allusive and Jamesian—and hardly anyone with a firmer sense of melodramatic plot or a more vigorous gift of storytelling."
                                    —Anthony Boucher, *The New York Times*

THE LONG FAREWELL   P 575, $2.40
"A model of the deft, classic detective story, told in the most wittily diverting prose."   —*The New York Times*

THE MAN FROM THE SEA   P 591, $2.84
"The pace is brisk, the adventures exciting and excitingly told, and above all he keeps to the very end the interesting ambiguity of the man from the sea."   —*New Statesman*

THE SECRET VANGUARD   P 584, $2.84
"Innes . . . has mastered the art of swift, exciting and well-organized narrative."   —*The New York Times*

THE WEIGHT OF THE EVIDENCE   P 633, $2.84
"First-class puzzle, deftly solved. University background interesting and amusing."   —*Saturday Review of Literature*

Mary Kelly

THE SPOILT KILL   P 565, $2.40

"Mary Kelly is a new Dorothy Sayers. . . . [An] exciting new novel."
                                                    —*Evening News*

Lange Lewis

THE BIRTHDAY MURDER   P 518, $1.95

"Almost perfect in its playlike purity and delightful prose."
                                —Jacques Barzun and Wendell Hertig Taylor

Allan MacKinnon

HOUSE OF DARKNESS   P 582, $2.84

"His best . . . a perfect compendium."
        —Jacques Barzun & Wendell Hertig Taylor, *A Catalogue of Crime*

Arthur Maling

LUCKY DEVIL   P 482, $1.95

"The plot unravels at a fast clip, the writing is breezy and Maling's
approach is as fresh as today's stockmarket quotes."
                                        —*Louisville Courier Journal*

RIPOFF   P 483, $1.95

"A swiftly paced story of today's big business is larded with intrigue as
a Ralph Nader-type investigates an insurance scandal and is soon on the
run from a hired gun and his brother. . . . Engrossing and credible."
                                                        —*Booklist*

SCHROEDER'S GAME   P 484, $1.95

"As the title indicates, this Schroeder is up to something, and the un-
ravelling of his game is a diverting and sufficiently blood-soaked entertainment."   —*The New Yorker*

Austin Ripley

MINUTE MYSTERIES   P 387, $2.50

More than one hundred of the world's shortest detective stories. Only
one possible solution to each case!

Thomas Sterling

THE EVIL OF THE DAY   P 529, $2.50

"Prose as witty and subtle as it is sharp and clear. . .characters unconven-
tionally conceived and richly bodied forth . . . . In short, a novel to be
treasured."   —Anthony Boucher, *The New York Times*

Henry Wade (cont'd)

THE HANGING CAPTAIN   P 548, $2.50

"This is a detective story for connoisseurs, for those who value clear thinking and good writing above mere ingenuity and easy thrills."

        —*Times Literary Supplement*

Hillary Waugh

LAST SEEN WEARING . . .   P 552, $2.40

"A brilliant tour de force."   —Julian Symons

THE MISSING MAN   P 553, $2.40

"The quiet detailed police work of Chief Fred C. Fellows, Stockford, Conn., is at its best in *The Missing Man* . . . one of the Chief's toughest cases and one of the best handled."

      —Anthony Boucher, *The New York Times Book Review*

Henry Kitchell Webster

WHO IS THE NEXT?   P 539, $2.25

"A double murder, private-plane piloting, a neat impersonation, and a delicate courtship are adroitly combined by a writer who knows how to use the language."   —Jacques Barzun and Wendell Hertig Taylor

Anna Mary Wells

MURDERER'S CHOICE   P 534, $2.50

"Good writing, ample action, and excellent character work."

      —*Saturday Review of Literature*

A TALENT FOR MURDER   P 535, $2.25

"The discovery of the villain is a decided shock."   —*Books*

Edward Young

THE FIFTH PASSENGER   P 544, $2.25

"Clever and adroit . . . excellent thriller . . ."   —*Library Journal*

If you enjoyed this book you'll want to know about
THE PERENNIAL LIBRARY MYSTERY SERIES

Buy them at your local bookstore or use this coupon for ordering:

Qty	P number	Price
___	___	___
___	___	___
___	___	___
___	___	___
___	___	___
___	___	___
___	___	___
___	___	___
___	___	___
___	___	___
___	___	___
___	___	___
___	___	___

	postage and handling charge	$1.00
___	book(s) @ $0.25	___
	TOTAL	_____

Prices contained in this coupon are Harper & Row invoice prices only.
They are subject to change without notice, and in no way reflect the prices at
which these books may be sold by other suppliers.

**HARPER & ROW, Mail Order Dept. #PMS, 10 East 53rd St., New
York, N.Y. 10022.**

Please send me the books I have checked above. I am enclosing $_____
which includes a postage and handling charge of $1.00 for the first book and
25¢ for each additional book. Send check or money order. No cash or
C.O.D.s please

Name_____

Address_____

City_____ State_____ Zip_____

Please allow 4 weeks for delivery. USA only. This offer expires 4-30-84.
Please add applicable sales tax.